"If you hadn't seen that guy and tackled me like that, I'd have been blown to bits, wouldn't I?"

"Probably." They'd been lucky that the restaurant's tables were old and heavy and made of solid wood. That fact alone had likely saved both of their lives.

He reached over and took her hands in his. He looked her directly in the eye. "Thank you," he said simply.

"You're welcome." Their gazes met and touched in a moment of naked honesty. They were *alive*. Such a simple thing but so very precious. He reached up slowly with one hand to touch her cheek. A light touch. Just the tips of his fingers trailing across her cheekbone and tracing the line of her jaw. A shiver passed through her and a single, errant thought filled her mind. *Do that again.*

He murmured, "A woman who can dance like you shouldn't also be some sort of super-spy."

"Why not?" she breathed back. His gaze was mesmerizing, probing hers with an intelligence that made her worry about how much he was seeing of her.

"It's too much. You're intimidating."

Dear Reader,

I have a confession to make before you read this story. I was, indeed, a professional Middle Eastern dancer for years. I'm sure I was never quite as beautiful or talented as my latest Medusa, Casey Chandler is, though!

I encourage you to go see a Middle Eastern dancer perform near you sometime. It's a spectacular art form, and the innovations going on within the dance today are nothing short of amazing. What I love best about it is that every woman (and men, too), no matter what their age, shape or size, looks beautiful and powerful and free when they belly dance.

And isn't that what the message of the Medusas has always been—that any woman can do anything she wants to if she sets her mind and heart to it, be it saving the world or finding true love? So sit back, put on a little music and enjoy Casey's story as she does both!

All my best,

Cindy

CINDY DEES

Medusa's Sheik

ROMANTIC

SUSPENSE

SILHOUETTE BOOKS

Recycling programs for this product may not exist in your area.

ISBN-13: 978-0-373-27703-2

MEDUSA'S SHEIK

CINDY DEES

started flying airplanes while sitting in her dad's lap at the age of three and got a pilot's license before she got a driver's license. At age fifteen, she dropped out of high school and left the horse farm in Michigan, where she grew up, to attend the University of Michigan.

After earning a degree in Russian and East European studies, she joined the U.S. Air Force and became the youngest female pilot in its history. She flew supersonic jets, VIP airlift and the C-5 Galaxy, the world's largest airplane. She also worked part-time gathering intelligence. During her military career, she traveled to forty countries on five continents, was detained by the KGB and East German secret police, got shot at, flew in the first Gulf War, met her husband and amassed a lifetime's worth of war stories.

Her hobbies include professional Middle Eastern dancing, Japanese gardening and medieval reenacting. She started writing on a one-dollar bet with her mother and was thrilled to win that bet with the publication of her first book in 2001. She loves to hear from readers and can be contacted at www.cindydees.com.

How could this book be dedicated to anyone other than my Middle Eastern Dance instructors over the years, women who preserve and share this ancient art form and make it new again? With each generation of dancers who are trained, the great sisterhood of women spanning the history of mankind expands and grows, and that's a beautiful thing.

So thanks to Trudi, Isis, Vashti, Tambra, Karen B., Suhaila and so many other magnificent ladies. Dance on!

Chapter 1

Hakim El Aran, "Hake" to his British friends, took the flavored rose water and soda from the waitress. He sipped it before turning to his lawyer, Geoffrey Birch. "So, have you come up with a solution to my problem?"

The older man gave a noncommittal shrug. "Let's talk business after the show." He reached for a menu. "Food's excellent here, by the by."

"When did you develop a taste for Middle Eastern food?"

"Since I saw the entertainment that comes with it."

Amusement bordering on disbelief crept into Hake's voice. "You mean the belly dancer?" He had serious trouble picturing strait-laced Birch enjoying the gyrations of some half-naked female along with his dinner.

The lawyer explained earnestly, "This isn't just any belly dancer. It's Cassandra. She's amazing."

On cue, the overhead lights dimmed in the packed

restaurant, while Hake stared at his companion. Geoffrey lived and breathed for the law. Hake had never seen anyone or anything that could distract him from his work. But apparently, this Cassandra chick had pulled off the impossible. The woman's timing couldn't have been any worse.

Irked at the dancer sight unseen, Hake watched the center of the cavernous room, where five musicians sat on a raised platform behind a parquet stage. He'd traveled with his father since he was a small boy, and he'd seen the greatest belly dancers in the world from Cairo to California and back. He highly doubted some schlocky theme club in London had pulled in a top-flight performer. He braced himself for a travesty of actual Middle Eastern dance.

The overhead lights faded away to nothingness, and the background buzz quieted. Darkness, relieved only by the small candles at each table, cloaked the restaurant. The silence grew thick with anticipation. Scents of cumin and cinnamon swirled around Hake, accompanied by the musky tang of Turkish tobacco.

Middle Eastern music began to play almost subliminally quiet, gradually growing in volume. Hake was suddenly gripped by a sensation of approaching a giant bazaar from afar. It promised exotic sights and sounds, bright colors and a tangle of pungent odors. *Home.*

Not that he'd been home to Bhoukar in years. His work abroad for his father, and El Aran Industries, kept him on the move. Truth be told, he'd been avoiding going home most of that time. He was deep into prime marriageable age, and he had no interest in dealing with scheming aunties and the political jockeying of people trying to ally themselves to the powerful El Aran family. But the marriage trap was closing in on him fast. Hence, tonight's meeting with his attorney.

Into the restaurant's gloom, a lone spotlight illuminated. It cast a bright circle in the center of the stage, bathing the spot in harsh, desert brilliance. A haze of smoke wafted through the column of light. The music pulsed rhythmically, gaining power with every beat. Despite his cynicism, he had to admit a certain visceral excitement rose in his gut. Maybe it was the call of the desert to his half-Saracen blood.

A dancer glided into the shimmering mirage of light as if conjured from the heat and smoke. Slender and darkly, ravishingly beautiful, she wore a costume dripping with red, glittering beads that caressed her golden skin and glowed against her raven hair. Hake stared in appreciation. She looked the part at any rate.

Eyes closed, her arms open in sensual invitation, she swayed with the music. The melody caressed the dancer, a feather drawn across her skin with a loving hand. She shivered at its delicate touch. Something about her called to Hake, beguiling and beckoning him—something beyond the obvious sexual allure of a beautiful, scantily clad woman. She was the music and the music was her soul.

The outside world ceased to exist as he was drawn into her dance. The moment contained only the woman, the music and him. Her body glistened with a sheen of perspiration as she undulated for him, her movements an extension of the mysterious *taksim* melody twining about them both.

His avid gaze followed a ripple which started just below her ribs, traveling sinuously down her stomach to the top of the heavily fringed belt that rode low on her hips. The belly roll traveled back up her torso, leading his gaze to the plunging, crystal-encrusted bra that revealed a cleft of swelling softness.

Her figure was an exquisite hourglass of perfectly

toned muscle. As a nearly invisible hip vibration caused the dancer's fringe to quiver against her skin, he was struck by an urge to feel her doing that beneath him, gripping his male flesh in building ecstasy.

She sank slowly to the floor, her arms rolling elegantly, as if they rested on the surface of a gently swelling ocean. One movement flowed seamlessly into the next as the dancer rose again, invoking images of a snake rising charmed out of its basket—graceful, exotic and mesmerizing.

It was probably rude to stare at her as if he were intent upon devouring her, but he couldn't stop himself. She was stunning. Her control—of both her muscles and the moment—was exquisite. The drums quieted to an erotic throbbing and her head fell back, exposing the artful line of her throat. Potent sexuality poured off her along with the heat of her body, steamy and tangible in the restaurant's dim light.

Hake shifted uncomfortably, his body raging in response to the woman before him. Her smoky sensuality enveloped him like a silken veil. He felt a strange intimacy with the dancer, as if he knew her somehow, as if she were dancing just for him. He studied her sculpted features, the straight, narrow nose framed by wide, catlike eyes, the high cheekbones, the delicately defined jaw.

No wonder Geoffrey had gone loopy over her. Hake managed to wrest his gaze away from the dancer long enough to glance at his dinner companion. The attorney stared slack-jawed at the woman. Hake felt a little better as he scanned the crowded restaurant. Everyone, it seemed, was caught in her thrall. Even the waiters stood motionless by the kitchen doors, transfixed by the dancer's magic.

Effortlessly, spectacularly, she had woven a web around the room. She'd transported them all to a faraway fantasy of hot desert winds and the sumptuous splendors of a seraglio, to a place where women such as her existed solely for the pleasure of the men who owned them.

As drums joined the strains of dusty flute music, the tempo increased and the mood changed in an instant. The dancer's head snapped forward and her eyes flashed open, fiery with passion. As it so happened, she was facing Hake directly when she did it. Her gaze speared into him.

They both froze. She, too, seemed caught in the grip of a powerful, instinctive recognition. Something alive coiled between them, pulling them inexorably toward one another. Sudden knowing burst across him. *This woman was meant to be his.*

Buried somewhere in the back of his brain, a sarcastic internal voice commented that his family would just love it if he brought home a belly dancer he'd met in a tawdry joint in London. In conservative quarters of Middle Eastern culture, dancers were often viewed as barely one step above prostitutes. But insatiable need to have this woman, to mark her as his, overwhelmed all else.

For an endless, breathless moment, the music paused while the dancer stared at him, the connection between them naked in her gaze.

She was his.

Casey Chandler stared at the man in devastating shock. The music faded and the spotlights spun around the edges of her vision.

It was *him.*

Hakim El Aran.

The one face she emphatically didn't want to see here tonight. She was supposed to make contact with his lawyer, not with the suspect himself.

El Aran's intent gaze touched her physically, sliding across her skin like a lover's cajoling caress, willing her to come to him, threatening to strip away the layers of her deceit. All of a sudden, she felt naked. Exposed far beyond the skimpiness of her costume.

Her breathing faltered and betraying heat flared low in her abdomen. Sizzling awareness tingled in her toes and raced like lightning to the tips of her fingers. *Focus.* She was on the *job!* Men weren't supposed to have this effect on her when she was working. Particularly not this one. She'd been warned that he was a ladies' man. but she'd never dreamed he'd be like this.

She was a soldier, for goodness' sake. A trained Special Forces operative working undercover. Not a harem girl swept off her feet by the first come-hither glance some Arab prince threw at her. Although technically, he was Bhoukari, from the small principality nestled between Oman and Yemen. And technically, he was only a sheik— several dozen cousins away from being emir of Bhoukar. Still. She was not supposed to react to him like this!

Tell that to her body. Her flesh throbbed with need, tingling as if he were already drawing his fingers across her skin, already whispering for her to dance the oldest dance of all for him. He wasn't a ladies' man. He was a lady killer.

The drummer gave a sharp pop on his *tabla,* the ceramic drum perched between his knees, demanding her attention. Awareness of her surroundings returned abruptly. Good Lord. She'd stopped dancing cold in front of a restaurant full of people, in the middle of a song, no less. She threw an apologetic glance over her shoulder at the musicians and picked up the rhythm of the music with her finger cymbals.

She moved to the other side of the stage, carefully avoiding glancing in *his* direction. Thing was, to do the dance justice, she had to put her heart into her performance.

Share a little piece of her soul with the audience. It simply was not possible for her to dance and maintain military detachment simultaneously.

It was terribly dangerous for him to see her like this. The next time they met, he might recognize her. And that could be disastrous. One word from Hake to the wrong people and the whole mission would come crashing down around her.

While most of her mind concentrated on the performance, a tiny piece of it prayed desperately that she'd make it offstage before disaster struck. She had to think. Had to figure out what to do, how to respond, how to salvage the mission.

Panic tickled the edges of her consciousness, but blessedly, her training and the performer within her knew how to cope. She concentrated on breathing, then on moving her feet, and then on relaxing her shoulders. The show continued, but her mind ran unchecked, leaping from one disjointed thought to another.

Why, oh why, did he have to show up now? She was a week at most from convincing Birch to hand over the evidence on the El Aran empire. Should she still try to talk to Birch tonight? Or maybe she should delay until the next time he showed up here. Except that could be days or weeks from now. Did she dare wait that long? The Medusas' other intelligence sources were hinting that there might not be much time left before Hake and his father made the sale of nuclear production equipment to an unnamed buyer.

Could she skip the attorney and play the son directly? Did she dare?

It would be a dangerous gambit. By all accounts, Hake was smart, suspicious and wary of women. But then, why wouldn't he be? Available, gorgeous females went into mass feeding frenzies any time he went out in public. It must really suck for him, being a billionaire, single, handsome and under the age of forty.

No, it wouldn't work. She'd never get close enough to him to find out what he was up to. And frankly, she'd be damned if she'd throw herself at any man, mission or no mission. The only way for a seduction of Hake El Aran to work would be for him to approach her. And that wasn't going to happen in this lifetime.

The rest of the show passed in a blur. She was vaguely aware of the audience's enthusiastic applause, the Middle Eastern customers shouting, *"Aiwa, habibi!"* Technically, it meant "Yes, darling," but a better translation was probably "Yeah, baby!"

She made her exit, gliding through the kitchen doors. The minute they swung shut behind her, she picked up her skirts and fled down the long hallway to her dressing room. She collapsed onto the stool at her makeup table and stared at her reflection in the lighted mirror. Beneath her airbrushed tan, she was pale as a ghost. She pressed icy palms to her cheeks.

What the hell had happened to her out there? As the Brits like to put it, the guy'd gobsmacked her but good. One look from Hake El Aran and she was a mess. *Get a grip. You're a trained killer.* Not that she'd been out on all that many missions, but she wasn't a complete idiot. Except when it came to hunky sheiks, apparently.

He made her feel like a…a woman. And in her world, that was emphatically not a good thing. She was the job. The next military mission to save the world. She did not do girly stuff, particularly if it involved emotions, swooning over men, or—heaven forbid—makeup. The sexy costume and heavy, cat-eyed stage makeup she wore tonight, notwithstanding. That stuff was all a disguise. None of it was *her*.

Then why was she such a basket case all of a sudden? Where were her vaunted Medusa nerves of steel? Bizarre how she was as calm as a cucumber when someone was shooting at her. But let Hake El Aran turn on the charm, and she fell completely apart.

She'd been shocked, and frankly, none too pleased, when her boss, Lt. Colonel Vanessa Blake, had briefed her on this mission and the need for her skill as a Middle Eastern dancer. She'd always done it for the exercise, not because she wanted to be Mata Hari someday. But like she'd verified for Vanessa, it took years, decades even, to train a world-class Middle Eastern dancer. Furthermore, it was not an art that could be faked in front of a knowledgeable audience. Hence her being here. Half-naked, slathered in makeup, perfume and hair spray, dancing in a nightclub.

None of this was real. She was just bait. Darned successful bait, it turned out. She'd been trying to net the minnow but had hooked the shark, apparently.

In her defense, she hadn't been expecting Hake, nor for him to look at her like that. Plus, when she danced she let down her emotional defenses. Like it or not, to do the dance justice she had to tap heavily into her feminine side. One thing she knew for sure, she could never, ever confess her reaction to Hake to her teammates. They'd never let her hear the end of it.

Faced with the horrifying truth that she was desperately attracted to the man she was supposed to take down, only one question remained: if she actually managed to reel in the shark, what on earth was she going to do with him?

Chapter 2

Hake contemplated Birch, who sipped at a tiny glass of arrack, the potent, licorice-flavored liqueur of the Middle East. He noted Geoffrey's flush, the subtle shifting in his seat, the uncharacteristic silence. Hake's mouth twitched in amusement. The dancer had seriously affected the poor man. He took pity and laid down his napkin beside his plate.

"When you called, you said you'd researched my situation. Have you figured out a way to deal with it?"

The attorney leaned forward, abruptly serious, abruptly at work. "You realize, of course, that this conversation is completely off the record. I'll deny any knowledge of it if you repeat a word of it."

Hake leaned forward, equally serious. "Cut the lawyer crap. It's me you're talking to, old friend. You've known my father since before I was born and watched me grow up. You know I won't say anything."

"Yes, but I am counsel to your father as well, and you're asking me to advise you against him. It's a blatant conflict of interest to involve myself in a dispute between the two of you."

"Fine. I have duly noted that this conversation is off the record."

The attorney's shoulders relaxed fractionally.

"So tell me, Geoffrey, hypothetically of course, if you weren't my father's attorney and represented only me, what would you advise me to do? Is he within his rights to insist I get married before he'll release my trust fund to me?"

"More or less."

"Don't equivocate. Yes or no?"

"Marriage is not stipulated in the terms of the trust, but there is a clause stating that your father must approve the release of the funds. In reality, he can set whatever conditions he wants before he'll give you that approval."

Hake's jaw tightened into the rippling mass of tension that never failed to make people around him jumpy on the rare occasions it occurred. Although quiet, his voice vibrated with fury. "What the hell am I supposed to do?"

"I'd suggest, my dear boy, that you start looking for a wife. Although I do have to ask, why do you want your trust released to you? You have millions in other funds. Money that you've earned for yourself."

In truth, it was the principle of the thing getting under his skin. He didn't like the idea of anyone else having control over him in any way. "So I've got to do the wife thing, huh?" Hake remarked grimly.

"It wouldn't be the end of the world. You might even discover you like it."

"You're a fine one to talk. I don't see you breaking your neck racing to the altar."

Geoffrey grinned unrepentantly. "Nobody's forcing me

into it. Frankly, I think your father secretly detests lawyers. He doesn't want to encourage us to reproduce."

"Lucky dog."

Geoffrey smiled and glanced over at the stage where Cassandra had performed. Hake was startled by an urge to grit his teeth in response. "Has my father indicated how soon he expects me to marry?"

"My impression is that he'd like the matter settled within a year."

"A year?" Hake echoed in dismay. If his old man wanted him to marry, Hake suspected there wasn't going to be a whole hell of a lot he could do to stop it. But the thought infuriated him. He was thirty-five years old, had already made his own millions, and was his own man, dammit. It was high time his father recognized that he was an adult, full-grown and capable of running his own life, including marrying or not marrying. Personally, he voted for the not-marrying option. There were so many beautiful women out there. Why be in any rush to close the door on them all?

Geoffrey asked, "Are you seeing anyone right now?"

Hake kept his expression bland. He'd lay odds his father had instructed the lawyer to ask that question. He answered vaguely, "I see a few women here and there."

He dated any number of women casually, but none held his attention for long. At the end of the day, they were all pretty much the same. They wanted the same things, were impressed by the same things, reacted the same way in most situations. Although he enjoyed having a beautiful one around for decoration and taking advantage of the pleasures one could offer, he didn't particularly *need* women. And that was the main reason he'd never married. Why saddle himself with someone who would ultimately become an inconvenience?

"Hake, now may be your only chance to choose your

own wife before your father gets involved and chooses one for you. I hate to say it, but if I were you, I'd start hunting for a nice girl who doesn't make you crazy. You know as well as I do your father's not going to budge on this."

Hake restrained an urge to swear.

Birch continued, "I never thought I'd hear myself say this, but if I were you, I might seriously consider finding a woman who will agree to be your wife in return for... some sort of compensation."

"You're saying I should *buy* a wife? You don't think I can get a woman to agree to marry me on my own merits?" Hake was genuinely shocked. He literally had to fight off women. He didn't need to buy one. Hell, all he had to do was hold out a diamond ring and they'd be falling over each other to snatch it.

Geoffrey squirmed uncomfortably. "I was thinking more along the lines of...a marriage of...convenience. Something mutually beneficial to both of you."

Hake sat back in his chair, flabbergasted. "You're joking."

"You could dictate the conditions of the relationship to your liking. After she produces an heir, you might want the freedom to maintain...discreet liaisons...on the side, maybe separate residences for the two of you, that sort of thing."

"What am I supposed to do? Walk up to..." Hake cast around for a suitably outrageous example "...say, that dancer we just saw, and ask her to marry me? I'll put her up in the lap of luxury forever in return for her marrying me, making a baby or two, and then leaving me the hell alone for the rest of my life? You've lost your mind!"

Geoffrey shrugged and grinned. "You're right. Forget I mentioned it. It was a ridiculous notion." He picked up his glass. "A toast. To bachelorhood."

Hake matched the lawyer's grin and clinked glasses with Geoffrey. "To bachelorhood."

Maneuvering awkwardly in the small space of her dressing room, Casey removed the heavy, beaded costume and hung it up to dry. Wrapped in a thin cotton robe, she fanned herself until she cooled down and then began repairing her stage makeup. Despite all of it being heavy-duty and waterproof, it was simply not possible to keep makeup entirely in place as she sweated profusely over the course of a forty-five-minute show. There was no getting around it. Belly dancing was strenuous stuff.

She sipped at a bottle of water to rehydrate before the next show in about an hour. Right before she went on, she would eat a tablespoon of peanut butter. She needed the calories and protein to get through another forty-five minutes of aerobic exertion. On performance days, she didn't eat after breakfast and wouldn't eat again until after her second and final show. A large meal would make her stomach stick out and not have the smooth, sinuous line customers associated with Middle Eastern dancers.

She had some time to spare before she needed to put on her next costume. Idly, she unlocked her equipment bag and checked her service pistol, ammunition clips and various other tools of the Special Forces trade that she currently had stowed along with spare finger cymbals, music CDs and safety pins.

Out of habit, she checked her cell phone for messages. None. Her headquarters, H.O.T. Watch Ops, was aware of this show. Heck, knowing that gang, they had a surveillance camera somewhere in the restaurant. She could just picture the cave full of analysts and Special Forces operatives getting a cheap thrill watching her dance. She hoped they all were too uncomfortable to stand up straight. It would serve them right.

She glanced in the mirror and met her own cold, cynical gaze with a certain relief. "Welcome back, Captain Chandler," she muttered. Who was she kidding? A special operator like her could never land a man like Hake El Aran. He'd take one look into her hard-edged gaze and run screaming.

It wasn't that she hated men. Far from it. It was just that she was entirely realistic about her inadequacies when it came to dealing with all things pertaining to men. She didn't do the girly thing well, she didn't do the girl-boy thing well either. Take Hake, for example. The guy was smoking-hot and she definitely felt intense attraction to him. But the idea of acting on her impulses struck terror into her heart.

Nope, a direct approach to the El Aran heir definitely was out of the question. She would continue with the original plan and focus her attention upon the manufacturing empire's much more gullible attorney. It wasn't as if she was asking Birch to violate attorney-client privilege. She was merely urging him to assist in a vital, joint undercover operation between the United States and Great Britain by giving them advance notice of the timing of a business deal.

Geoffrey Birch was an honorable and patriotic man. He would do the right thing for Crown and country. This mission would be a piece of cake. And then she'd get on with her regularly scheduled life and Hake El Aran could get on with whatever it was that he did.

"Miss Cassandra?" one of the waiters called through her door. "A man. He wishes to meet you."

"You know my policy on that, Ismael. I don't chat up the patrons and I don't allow men in my dressing room."

"He is most insistent, ma'am. He offered me a thousand pounds to introduce him to you." A pause. "I could really use the money. My wife is pregnant—"

Oh, for crying out loud. A thousand pounds? She tried to guess which one it was. The restaurant had been packed with middle-aged, successful-looking businessmen. No telling which one had made the outrageous offer. And frankly, she wasn't the slightest bit curious to find out. Men were all pretty much the same around belly dancers. They thought they could take liberties and make offensive suggestions because they'd seen a girl half-naked and sharing her most sensual self with him…and everyone else in the joint. But that last bit always seemed to escape the pushy patrons.

She did hate to cost the waiter that much cash, though. Her gaze glittered with irritation in the mirror. She called out, "Fine. Tell him he can buy me a drink after my second show. But make sure he pays up first."

Ismael called back his enthusiastic thanks, and she was alone again. She remembered now why she'd never pursued a full-time career as a dancer. She adored the music, and there was nothing quite like the exhilaration of feeling the rhythms of it moving through her, shaping her body and freeing her soul to fly. It was just that she couldn't deal with the men. Good thing she worked with all women on Medusa Team Two.

When Geoffrey excused himself to go to the loo, Hake had a quiet word with the maître d'. A wad of cash changed hands and Hake leaned back more relaxed than he'd been since that dancer had shocked him to his toes earlier.

Birch returned to the table. Hake announced jovially, "Well, old man, you and I both have plenty of work to do tomorrow. What say we call it a night?"

Geoffrey looked wistfully at the empty stage and nodded reluctantly. "Yes, of course. You're right. Too bad Cassandra didn't come out to say hello to the patrons tonight."

Hake's mouth turned down sardonically. "If I were her, I might not show myself either. With the state she got this crowd worked up into, she'd run a real risk of being assaulted."

Geoffrey smiled, a tight, smug little smile. "Indeed. And besides, there are so many better ways to make contact with a woman than mugging her in a place like this."

Hake's gaze snapped to his lawyer. Now what did the old bird mean by that? Did the man actually have aspirations of meeting the divine Cassandra and having her for himself? A stab of something sharp and unpleasant speared through Hake's gut. What was that all about? How odd.

He escorted the attorney from the restaurant and hailed a cab for the man. As soon as the black taxi had disappeared around the corner, Hake turned and headed back into the restaurant. The maître d' had been more than happy to hold his table for him—for a hefty tip, of course. Hake ordered himself a drink and sat back to anticipate the return of Cassandra to grace the stage and perform for him.

Casey peeked out of the kitchen moments before the lights were to dim, startled at how many patrons from the first show were still in the restaurant. And then she caught sight of *him*. Hake was still out there. By himself now, but squarely facing the stage and nursing a drink.

Butterflies leaped in her stomach. Usually, she experienced no stage fright at all. Yet the idea of Hake watching her again, observing every nuance of her body, made her all but hyperventilate. She glanced down at her costume, gold and skimpy and beaded from head to toe. In keeping with the later show, this costume showed more leg and cleavage and her arms were completely bare except for matching snake bracelets clasping her upper arms. She swore under her breath. She could really go for a set of full camouflage clothing right about now.

"Ready, Cassandra?" the manager murmured, startling her.

"Uh, yes. I guess so."

"Knock 'em dead, love. Not that you don't always. My receipts triple on the nights you dance."

She smiled gratefully at the manager, who was in on her secret identity and the reason for it. They'd needed him to shuffle the dancers' schedules around to accommodate adding Casey to the rotation, and he'd initially been reluctant, Scotland Yard request or no. It had threatened to turn into an ugly stalemate until she'd diplomatically suggested that maybe an audition for the man was in order. Of course, once she'd danced for him, he'd been more than happy to give her the coveted Saturday night shows.

The restaurant went black. The musicians started playing so softly she could barely hear them. She closed her eyes, let the exotic chords wash over her and through her, and Casey Chandler, former FBI agent and current Special Forces operative, retreated. Cassandra, the desert seductress, took over. *It's a disguise. Just a disguise.*

Without Birch present, Hake allowed himself to truly appreciate Cassandra's second show. If possible, it was even more sultry and alluring than the first. She really was an accomplished dancer. As fine as any he'd ever seen. They'd go crazy over her in Cairo, the global capital of belly dancing.

She aroused him so intensely that it would be a while before he could leave the table without embarrassing himself.

After the show, he kept an eagle eye on the kitchen from

whence she would emerge. He'd already ascertained from a helpful waiter that she was not married and, furthermore, never arrived or left the restaurant in the company of a gentleman. Fierce satisfaction coursed through him at that news. Nonetheless, Hake was determined not to let anyone else move in on her. And no way was he letting her slip past him and duck the drink she'd agreed to let him buy her. He wanted her and he planned to have her for himself. End of discussion.

Chapter 3

A hush fell over the cavernous interior of H.O.T. Watch headquarters and the nearly three dozen intelligence analysts, communications experts and Special Forces operatives clustered in the giant underground facility to watch Cassandra's second set in the nightclub. When it ended, Beau Breckenridge, one of the lead duty controllers murmured, "Whoa. That girl sure can dance."

The six women standing beside him all snorted, but the commander of the entire Medusa Project, Lt. Colonel Vanessa Blake, was the one to answer. "She's a Medusa. We do a thing well or we don't do it at all. I wouldn't have suggested her for this mission if I didn't know she was good."

Breckenridge grinned. "How long did it take her to learn to dance like that?"

Alexandra Rios, known to her teammates as Tarantula,

answered, "She says she's been at it for close to twenty years."

Naraya El Saad, the Medusa's resident mathematician and genius at large, piped up in her cultured accent, "Trust me. It's taken every bit of twenty years to achieve that level of mastery. I danced a bit when I was a little girl and what she does is a great deal harder than it looks."

Beau stared at the reserved Middle Eastern woman. "You can dance like that?"

Naraya laughed. "No, not even close. That's why she got sent on this mission and not me. The op called for a professional dancer, not an enthusiastic but untalented amateur."

Navy Commander Brady Hathaway, the man in charge of the bunker tonight, interrupted, "And speaking of the mission, what are we going to do about Hake El Aran? Not only has he seen Scorpion, but he's just spent the past hour studying her in excruciating detail. Is she blown or do we proceed with the operation? Thoughts, ladies?"

Vanessa, aka Viper, frowned. "It took us a great deal of maneuvering to get my operative placed close to the El Aran empire. Marat El Aran is an extremely cagey and cautious man. I don't think we have time to establish another undercover operator before the deal goes down, do we?"

Hathaway looked over at Beau, who replied, "Our source says the sale is set to happen within the month."

Vanessa asked grimly, "Any word yet on exactly who the buyer is?"

Beau shook his head. "Nope. That's why we need your girl. We need her to find out who and where and when so we can stop the deal before some terrorist group gets its hands on the capacity to manufacture precision nuclear weapon parts."

The Medusas traded long, silent looks among themselves, then Vanessa spoke for all of them. "I think we should leave her in place. It's a calculated risk, but the stakes are too high to do any less. If her contact ends up being Hake El Aran himself, so be it."

Beau glanced back up at the jumbo screen and the image of Hake El Aran shifting in his seat and staring at the door from which Scorpion would emerge shortly. "I wish your girl luck," he muttered. "Lord knows she's gonna need it to deal with him. He's infamous for hating government officials and loving the ladies."

Casey finished stripping off the heavy stage makeup and replaced it with more appropriate personal makeup. God bless Roxi—the Medusa's fashion stylist turned commando—wherever she was tonight. The woman was magic with cosmetics, hair and fashion and had put her through a crash course in all of the above before this mission.

Casey checked to make sure her purse was zipped, her pistol tucked into its hidden compartment. The purse was cleverly padded so someone touching the bag wouldn't see or feel the weapon nested inside. As she slung the strap over her shoulder, she felt the telltale vibration of her cell phone within it. She dug it out. "Hello?"

"Scorpion. Viper here. We noticed the wrinkle sitting stage left tonight."

Casey winced. So, H.O.T. Watch *did* have a camera in the restaurant. "Did the boys enjoy the show?"

Vanessa laughed. "Oh, yeah. You completely silenced them. Not a single wisecrack out of the lot of them. Never thought I'd see the day. Congratulations."

"Cool. Any advice on removing wrinkles?" Casey asked.

"We've talked it over and agree that you should feel free to pursue that avenue if you think it might turn out to be profitable. But it's your call whether or not you think it has potential."

Casey stared at her reflection in the mirror. She was suddenly a bit pale. She was greenlighted to pursue Hake El Aran himself? Her first impulse was to run far away and hide from the man and his aggressive sensuality.

He'd been sending her vibes so charged with sexual promise during the show that she'd had trouble keeping her knees from buckling. The heat he'd aroused in her had practically incinerated the stage. She'd never danced that intensely before, and the audience hadn't missed it. The crowd had been all but drooling collectively by the time the show ended. It was why she'd dawdled backstage afterward. She was hoping most of the patrons left before she had to go out and face them.

Not to mention she dreaded facing her thousand-pound paying patron after that steamy performance. It was one thing to put on a girly act from a distance and behind the protection of a costume and makeup. But it was another thing entirely to keep up the act face-to-face with a man, one-on-one. She never had been comfortable around men, but in this persona, she would be expected to be perfectly at ease with the whole beautiful-woman-who-men-fawn-over-all-the-time thing. She admitted it. She was a big fat chicken.

"You still there?" Vanessa asked in her ear.

"Yes, I'm here. Thinking. It's a bold idea to go directly for the El Aran heir. Risky."

"Agreed. Is it worth the risk?"

Keeping nuclear weapons out of the hands of terrorists? Unfortunately, that one was a no-brainer. It was worth a whole lot more than flirting with some guy who might be more than she could handle. Strike that. Who no doubt *would* be more than she could handle. But that was just her tough luck. She was Medusa and she had a job to do.

"You and I both know the answer to that question," she replied grimly.

Her boss asked soberly, "Can you handle it, Scorpion?"

Dammit. Was it that obvious to her teammates that she was completely ill at ease with herself as a woman and with men in general? She sighed. "I guess I'll just have to."

Vanessa chuckled. "Hey, it could be worse. He's yummy. Have fun."

"Whatever," Casey scowled. "Oh, and next time could you let me know when I'm on *Candid Camera?*"

"Sorry about that. I thought it might make you self-conscious, so I didn't mention it. I promise I'll tell you next time."

"Thanks."

"Good luck. I know you can do this."

Casey disconnected the call glumly. She could do something all right. But she wasn't at all sure it would include succeeding on the mission. If she was lucky, Hake was long gone from the restaurant and would never be back. The issue of dealing with him directly would be moot.

The waiter, Ismael, spoke outside her door. "The customer's waiting for you, Miss Cassandra. He's on the last stool at the far end of the bar."

"Got it. Did he pay you?"

"Yes, and a hundred extra because he was so pleased that I talked you into it."

Casey smiled gamely at the young man. At least one person was going home happy tonight. She took a deep breath, squared her shoulders and stepped out into the restaurant. She headed resolutely for the bar. One drink, a polite-but-firm refusal of the patron's advances and she'd be out of here.

She stopped in her tracks, staring at the last stool on the end. Ohcrap, ohcrap, ohcrap. The patron was Hake El Aran.

Hake's breath hitched when he caught sight of Cassandra walking toward him. Her dress was black, sleeveless, simple and sexy as hell. He'd expected the usual model's catwalk while she strutted her stuff for him, but was startled to see her striding forward confidently, athletically even. Odd.

She frowned when she spotted him, which startled him. Disappointed that he wasn't someone else? What was there to frown about? He was a good-looking man, well-educated, heir to a giant manufacturing empire and richer than one man had a right to be. There was no arrogance in the knowledge…it was just a fact.

"Good evening, Mister…" Cassandra said cautiously.

"El Aran. But you can call me Hake." Huh. She was American, judging by the accent. He hadn't expected that. She slid onto the bar stool beside him, her gaze roving around the room keenly. "Worried about something?" he murmured.

Her gaze snapped back to him. "No. Why do you ask?"

"You were searching for someone."

She looked at him in momentary noncomprehension. Then, "Oh, that's just a habit of mine. I like to know what and who is around me."

"Does that come from being afraid of free-handed patrons when you dance?"

She smiled, a tight little thing that stemmed from confidence and maybe a hint of disdain. "No, I'm not afraid of any patron. I can take care of myself, thank you."

Startled, he studied her anew. Was there more to this dancer than met the eye? Intrigued, he leaned forward. "Tell me about yourself."

She gazed at him levelly. "I agreed to have a drink with you, not share my life story."

"Ah, but I paid dearly for that drink. I think I've purchased a little more than just polite conversation, don't you?"

She gazed pointedly at the empty napkin in front of her by way of response. He laughed and signaled over the bartender. "Get the lady a…" He looked over her.

"A bottle of water and a club soda with a twist of lime," she finished.

"Nothing stronger than that?" he blurted.

"Were you hoping to get me drunk and take advantage of me, perchance?" she retorted.

Prickly, she was. But he supposed he couldn't blame her. She must get sick of men trying to crawl all over her. He grinned and murmured, "I don't usually have to get women drunk to get them in my bed."

She inhaled a sharp, satisfying little breath. So, she wasn't totally unaffected by him after all. His male ego felt much better and he settled in to be patient. The hunt was an art form at which he happened to excel.

When she opened the bottle of water and drank the whole thing down, he grinned. "Thirsty were you?"

She picked up the club soda and took a daintier sip of it. "I can lose up to ten pounds of water weight during a single show."

"You must be in pretty good shape to do that night in and night out."

Her eyes glinted with humor. "I've been known to work out a bit," she commented drily.

"It shows," he replied.

Her eyebrows shot up and he thought that was veiled disapproval in her gaze.

"Oh, come now. Surely you know how perfect a body you have. You're toned from head to foot."

She merely shrugged. He looked for some indication that she was offended or playing coy but saw neither. Strange. Most women craved hearing men tell them how beautiful and desirable they were. She seemed…disinterested in the subject.

"What do you like to talk about?" he asked.

She studied him for a long moment. "Do you seriously care? We both know what you want from me, and intellectually stimulating conversation is not it."

Direct, this beautiful creature. As stunning as she'd been in her stage makeup, he was coming to the conclusion he liked her better like this. Her skin was flawless, her natural coloring more delicate without the heavy makeup. Her eyes were rounder and bluer without the eyeliner, too. Softer. Yet more remote, somehow.

He swirled his brandy and took a slow, appreciative sip. Then he surprised himself by answering, "Actually, yes. I do care what you like to talk about. Tell me."

"Why?"

"I find you intriguing."

She leaned close to him and murmured gently, "That's what they all say, Mr. El Aran."

He recoiled, stung. She was lumping him with every other lounge lizard who'd ever come on to her? How dared she? He wasn't some common bloke looking to bed the closest hot female he could land. He frowned. All right. So his end goal might be the same in principle, but he was imminently more sophisticated in how he went about getting it than most men.

On the heels of his disgruntlement came a flare of

something sharp and hot in his gut. Foreign. What *was* that? He took several more sips of his drink before he put a name to it. Attraction. He was intensely interested in this woman and the challenge she posed. He *would* find a way to have her. That decision reaffirmed after talking to her, he turned his attention to achieving his goal.

"What do you like to do in your free time?" he asked.

She gave the question the same consideration she had all his other questions so far. "I'm not accustomed to having much free time, so that's hard to answer. I like all sorts of things, I suppose. Reading. Traveling. Pretty much any activity having to do with water."

"Do you sail?"

"Yes."

"Water ski?"

"Yes."

"Snow ski?"

She nodded. That might even be a hint of a smile in her eyes.

"What do you read?"

"Everything. Anything."

Encouraged by the roll he was on in getting her to share information, he continued his rapid-fire questions. "Fiction or nonfiction?"

"Both."

"London or Paris?"

"Mmm. Tough. I love them both."

"Beaches or mountains?"

"Gorgeous natural scenery in any form," she equivocated.

"Fair enough. Steak or seafood?"

"Steak."

"Milk chocolate or dark?"

"Dark."

He made a mental note of that. "Favorite color of rose?"

"Red."

He grinned. "Of course. The color of passion. Quiet dinner for two or a big party?"

"The quiet dinner. I get my fill of loud crowds dancing."

"Bottom or top?"

She froze. Gave him a cool, level look that made it clear he'd just crossed the line and she didn't appreciate it. The sharp pull of this startling woman intensified. He couldn't remember the last time a female had set a boundary with him like that. Mostly, they tripped all over themselves to offer him whatever he wanted.

"Sorry," he said forthrightly.

She nodded, accepting his apology matter-of-factly. Now *that* was decidedly not typical of any female he'd ever known. Who *was* this woman?

"Where do you come from?" he asked, burning with curiosity to know more about her.

"America."

"I could tell that from the accent. America's a big place. Where, specifically, do you call home?"

"My family moved around a lot when I was a kid."

"Brothers and sisters?"

"I prefer to live in the moment and not discuss my background."

He considered that rather cryptic nonanswer. Didn't want to talk about her past, eh? He could fix that. Geoffrey's law firm had an entire team of private investigators who could tell him everything he ever wanted to know about Cassandra's life.

"Another club soda?" he asked.

"No, thank you. I believe you only paid for the one drink."

"What is it about me you find so distasteful?" he burst out.

Her right eyebrow arched slightly. "I don't find you distasteful, Mr. El Aran."

"Call me Hake," he all but snapped in his frustration at his failure to dazzle her.

She answered blandly, "I don't find you distasteful, Hake."

How did she manage to make him feel so stupid for his outburst like that? He took a deep breath. She was unpredictable, that was all. She didn't respond to anything like he expected her to. It was as if she was onto his game and determined to disrupt his usual pattern of the hunt. She was succeeding, too. He had no idea how to proceed with getting her into his bed at this point.

"What's your last name?" he asked in a certain desperation.

She smiled wryly. "I believe the correct answer to that one is, whatever you want it to be…Hake."

He rolled his eyes. "You're an exasperating woman, Cassandra."

She smiled in genuine amusement as if that had been her goal all along. Minx! "What am I going to do with you?" he muttered.

"That's easy," she replied lightly. "Nothing at all."

He looked at her directly, capturing her light gaze with his own dark one. "I think not, clever Cassandra. That's the one thing I'm definitely not going to settle for. You can fight me or tease me or try to run away from me, but I guarantee you I'm not going to settle for *nothing* from you."

Chapter 4

Casey mentally gulped. Beneath her devil-may-care exterior, she felt way over her head. She was definitely tempting fate to tangle with this man. His technique when it came to sweeping a girl off her feet was darned near perfect. Heck, it was hard to even look at him without getting a little breathless. There was handsome, and then there was drop-dead gorgeous. Hake fell somewhere beyond the latter. His eyes and hair were dark, but his skin reflected his mother's Caucasian heritage and bone structure.

And then there was the way he looked at her. Intently. With total focus. As if she was the most important person in the world. It was a heady thing to have this man's undivided attention. His verbal repartee was nothing to sneeze at either. He had her ducking and dodging like a prizefighter. But her instincts told her not to reveal herself to this man lest he take advantage of the smallest opening and strip her soul bare.

She expected someone in H.O.T. Watch Ops could read lips, assuming the gang there didn't have an audio feed of this conversation somehow. They must be in transports of ecstasy over how the encounter was going. She hadn't set out to play hard to get, but she couldn't help herself. She felt like a mouse being stalked by a tiger. Her years of Medusa training had taken over and she'd reflexively scrambled to deflect the predator coming after her. Just her luck, the tactic had made him even more eager to snare her.

From an operational perspective, that was fantastic. But from a personal one…the danger was almost more than she could face calmly. She sensed that this man had enormous power to hurt her. He would get inside her guard, and as sure as the sun rose and set, he'd break her heart.

She had to get away from him. She still had Geoffrey Birch. She didn't need this lethal man to complete her mission. She started to push back from the bar. "Thank you for the drink, but—"

It wasn't Hake who cut her off. Rather, it was her stomach. Growling loudly.

Her companion grinned. "Hungry?"

She shrugged, embarrassed. "I can't eat for twelve hours or so before I dance."

"And here I've been keeping you from your dinner!" he exclaimed. "How rude of me. Let me make it up and take you to dinner."

"No, thank you—"

He interrupted briskly. "I'm not taking no for an answer." He pulled out his cell phone, punched a button and spoke into it briefly. "My car will be around front momentarily." He tossed down a hefty tip for the bartender and reached courteously for her elbow. "Shall we?"

"I'm not having dinner with you!"

"Why not? You're hungry. I'm hungry. We both have to eat. Why not do it together?"

She couldn't very well confess that she was freaked out by all his questions and curiosity—and sheer male presence. While she tried to come up with a suitable answer, he steered her to the front door of the club. The night was damp and cool and shocked her into action.

"Hake. You can't do this. I don't want to—"

"Why not? You already said you don't find me distasteful. You're not afraid of me, are you? Afraid of how I make you feel, perhaps?"

He asked the latter with such obvious pleasure at the notion she couldn't admit he was exactly right. She was terrified of the things he did to her innards. She had no business whatsoever being attracted to him. He was a target. Nothing more.

"Here's the car," he announced cheerfully.

Calling the vehicle in front of her a car didn't do the glossy black Rolls-Royce any more justice than calling Hake handsome did for him. A uniformed chauffeur materialized in front of her, holding the back door open. "Mademoiselle," the man said politely.

To advance the mission, she had to go to dinner with Hake. This was just a job. Vanessa's doubtful question about whether or not she could handle it popped into her head, galling her. She *hated* the idea of being weak. She was a Medusa. She could handle one stinking meal with some hunky guy! The folks at H.O.T. Watch Ops would do back handsprings in delight if she went to dinner with the mark.

She smiled at the driver and stepped into the Rolls. It was as plush inside as it was outside. An elegant crystal bud vase was built into the armrest, and it held a single white rosebud.

"Champagne?" Hake murmured, reaching into the built in cooler.

"No, thank you." She never drank alcohol when she was armed and working. Besides, dealing with this man required every bit of her mental faculties.

He sighed. "You have nothing to be afraid of, Cassandra."

Given that she was trained in a dozen different methods of disabling him and probably twenty more ways of killing him, she would hardly call herself afraid. At least not of him directly. She was more afraid of herself. Of her reaction to him.

She slipped a hand into her purse and hit the speed-dial button that connected her to H.O.T. Watch Ops. Speaking loudly enough so the folks there could hear her over the smooth purr of the Rolls, she asked, "Where are we going for dinner?"

He smiled mysteriously. "It's a surprise."

She sighed. Oh, well. It had been worth a try. At least headquarters knew she would have dinner with the target. They could triangulate on the GPS unit in her cell phone if they wanted to see where she was going.

Hake leaned forward and opened the mini-refrigerator. He poured chilled water into a cut-crystal glass and held it out to her. "Here, my thirsty dancer."

She took the glass in silence. *His* dancer? The thought made her stomach tumble disconcertingly. *Stop that.* Not that her gut listened to her, of course.

"Is your dancing a safe topic?" he asked.

"I'll let you know," she replied cautiously.

He laughed quietly. "You are determined to lead me on a merry chase, aren't you?"

"I try."

The rest of the ride passed in silence. The Rolls headed

for the heart of London and took a street that ran along the Thames. The imposing medieval block of the Tower of London loomed across the river. And then the Rolls slowed and turned into a narrow, gated drive.

In a few minutes, the vehicle stopped. The chauffeur opened the door for her and Casey stepped out to see a pier with a half-dozen luxury yachts moored along its length. Hake held out his arm and she had no choice but to loop her fingers around his forearm.

The muscles beneath the fine wool suit were hard and sculpted. The guy worked out, did he? Her uncooperative stomach gave an appreciative flutter.

No surprise, he led her to the biggest, sleekest yacht of all. A white uniformed sailor, clearly also a highly trained bodyguard, welcomed Hake aboard. Casey recognized the sailor's relaxed, balanced stance as the same one she was trained to employ in high-threat security situations.

They passed two more crewmen on their way to the ship's expansive living room. Both men were as sharp as the first one. Of course, given Hake's wealth and prominence, it was no surprise he was surrounded by bodyguards of this caliber. Frankly, now that she thought about it, the biggest surprise was that these goons hadn't been with him at the restaurant.

She subtly slipped her hand in her purse and turned her phone on again. "What's this boat called?"

Hake grinned. "Don't call her a boat in the captain's presence unless you want a lecture. She's a yacht or a ship. And she's called the *Angelique*."

Mission accomplished. H.O.T. Watch's crack researchers would know where she was in two minutes, tops. She figured that in five more, they'd have satellite surveillance on her. Not that she needed the backup. She had things under control. At least for the moment.

A crewman came in and asked, "Are you ready to dine, sir?" At Hake's nod, the man laid a table for two. Hake spent the next few minutes giving her a tour of the salon, which held an impressive collection of art and baubles from around the world. Her host proved to have impressive expertise in both archaeology and art. In spite of herself, she wondered what else his wide-ranging education encompassed. She always had found smart men irresistible.

"Dinner is served," yet another crew member announced.

"How many people are on the *Angelique*'s crew?" she asked.

"Eleven at sea. Seventeen in port."

"Why the difference?"

"Security," he answered shortly. "My father insists upon it."

"He's probably right to insist," Casey commented before she stopped to think.

Hake whirled to stare at her. "You know who I am?"

Crap. She thought fast. Probably best to stick to the truth. "Of course, I know who you are. You're one of the most eligible bachelors in Europe. And with your... escapades...splashed all over the tabloids, it would be darn near impossible not to know who you are."

He rolled his eyes. "Don't believe most of what you read in the British gossip rags."

"The truth is worse?" she asked lightly.

Hake laughed. "If I were American, I'd plead the Fifth Amendment to that one."

She smiled. "I'll let you plead it...this time."

Hake waved off the crew member and held her chair for her himself. She brushed past him to take her seat and her pulse skittered at the proximity to him. Oh, Lord.

He smelled fabulous. His cologne was as smooth and sophisticated as he was.

Someone dimmed the lights in the salon, leaving only a pair of tall tapers between them for illumination. A low arrangement of a dozen red roses decorated the table. Was it just luck, or had he specifically ordered those flowers and his crew worked a miracle to get them at this time of night?

She looked down at her plate as the waiter uncovered it and had to smile. A gorgeous prime rib stared back up at her. "Your staff is really, really good," she commented wryly.

Hake merely smiled enigmatically at her and murmured, "Bon appétit."

The meal was delicious and the conversation enjoyable as they discussed everything from ballet to Formula 1 car racing—a hobby he'd given up recently at the worried urging of his family. Gradually, she found herself relaxing. It was just food and talk. She could handle those.

After a sumptuous dark chocolate mousse, she laid down her spoon with a sigh of contentment. "My compliments to the chef."

Hake nodded. "I'll pass them on."

She smiled over at him. "I have to confess, I've had a wonderful time. Although, I'm going to have to exercise for hours tomorrow to work that off." Thankfully, Hake didn't leap on that and suggest any lewd alternatives for working off the meal with him. She asked, "Would you have one of your men call me a cab, please?"

Hake looked stunned for a moment but recovered quickly. To his immense credit, he didn't argue or press her in any way to stay. He merely murmured, "No need for a cab. I'll have my driver take you home."

"I don't want to put him out," she protested. "It's very late."

Hake waved off her protest. "I insist. I'd worry about you making it home safely otherwise."

Right. As if she was in any danger. She highly doubted that too many people in London could hurt her in a one-on-one fight. She had to admit, though, another ride in that amazing Rolls would be fun. "All right," she acquiesced.

Hake walked her down the pier to the car a few minutes later. Although she was as nervous as a cat, he didn't even try to kiss her cheek good-night, and for that, she was grateful. Smart guy. Must have figured out his only chance was to go slow with her. Mental whiplash jerked her. His only chance? He had no chance at all with her. They were never going to be a couple or even hook up for a one-night stand. This was work.

"Thank you for a lovely evening," she murmured.

"Likewise. We must do it again soon."

Her toes curled at the prospect, but a frisson of alarm chattered down her spine. Too much more proximity to him and she'd be in grave danger of weakening.

She breathed a huge sigh of relief when she pulled away from the pier in his Rolls and his tall form faded into the night behind her. She gave an address to the driver and sat back to relish the plush seats and silky smooth ride.

The driver offered to walk her inside the apartment building but she turned him down firmly. She watched the vehicle until it had turned a corner up ahead and disappeared, then turned and flagged a taxi. She gave the driver, a grizzled Cockney fellow this time, her actual address and sat back for the long ride across London. She wasn't about to let Hake El Aran know where she was staying. After all, their relationship was going to end up being all about power and leverage if she didn't miss her guess.

Let him stew about how to get in touch with her again. He'd do it on her terms or not at all.

Chapter 5

Furious Hake leaned forward to glare at the pair of private investigators squirming in Geoffrey's office Monday afternoon. "What do you mean you've got nothing on her? Surely you managed to get her name at least!"

"I'm sorry, sir. The restaurant pays her in cash and she does business under a license in the name of Cassandra. Nothing more."

"My man told you where she lives from when he dropped her off. Couldn't you track her from that?"

Negative shakes of the P.I.s' heads. "False address. No woman matching her photograph lives in any apartment building for two blocks in any direction of the spot your man dropped her off."

Hake sat back, flabbergasted. The woman had well and truly hoodwinked him! She must be laughing her head off to have pulled the wool over his eyes like that. A part of him admired her clever evasion, but another was more determined than ever to solve the mystery of Cassandra. He knew one way to learn who she was. Ask the woman herself and don't let her off the hook until she told him what he wanted to know.

"When does she dance again?" he asked. "Did you at least find that out?"

The P.I.s looked relieved. "We did get that. This coming Saturday."

Five days until he could get to the bottom of this mystery. The wait would kill him. He tried not to look as if he was sulking, while Geoffrey dismissed the investigators and closed his office door behind them.

"Hake, you and I need to talk. I've got some news from your father."

When Geoffrey turned on the electronic white noise machine behind his desk to foil any possible listening devices, Hake sat up straight. Not many topics rated this level of caution from the attorney.

"The buyers have contacted your father and accepted his terms. The deal is a go."

"Excellent. What does he need me to do?" Hake replied, both appalled and relieved. He was appalled that he and his father were being forced into selling this equipment to likely terrorists and relieved that they might yet get out of this mess alive.

"Their agent will contact you here in London. Your father has one instruction for you—don't screw this up."

Hake snorted. "That goes without saying. Besides, I never screw up deals."

Geoffrey looked pained. "I really wish you two would reconsider this scheme. It's entirely too dangerous. There must be another way—"

Hake cut him off. "You have the affidavits from me

and my father on file, right? And copies elsewhere in safe deposit boxes?"

"Yes, yes. I followed all of your instructions to the letter. But as I've said before, I don't think a set of letters from you two stating that your intent is to identify these jokers and turn them over to the authorities once you have proof that they're trying to buy nuclear manufacturing equipment from you is going to hold up in court."

Hake sighed. They'd been over this before. "Geoffrey, my father and I are dead men if we refuse outright to do business with these people. They have the means and the mind-set to kill us simply because we know they exist. But no way is El Aran Industries selling precision milling machines to these madmen."

"Tell someone. Your own government. The Brits. The Americans. They'll help."

Mention of Americans sent Cassandra's lovely visage flashing through Hake's mind. Reluctantly, he pushed the image aside. "My father and I both agree that government bureaucracies would bumble around and mess up the deal. They'd end up getting us killed anyway. Better that we handle this on our own and turn over the bad guys when we have all the evidence we need to prove our innocence and good intentions."

"I don't like it," Geoffrey retorted heavily.

"Duly noted," Hake replied implacably. He didn't like it either, but what choice did they have? It was either appear to play ball with these terrorist, or be murdered. Personally, he richly appreciated being alive.

Hake spent much of the remainder of the week handling the paperwork associated with fabricating a state-of-the-art milling machine for an as-yet-unspecified buyer. He figured he would eventually have to come up with a fake entity to represent the real buyers. It would be the only way past the government regulators who closely watched such things. One step at a time, though. First he had to make contact with the terrorists and identify them. Then, he had to wait and see if they actually managed to come up with two million euros to pay for the machine.

Normally, he would've gone out and partied Friday night…and incidentally woken up Saturday morning to see himself on the front pages of the tabloids. But he was beat after a busy week of setting up the illegal deal and chose to go to the yacht to crash early and alone Friday evening.

He wasn't saving himself for Cassandra, dammit. He'd never limited himself to one woman, and he didn't plan to start now. He certainly didn't sit around mooning over some girl who hadn't even given him her name. He vowed grimly to have both her real name *and* a kiss from her tomorrow.

He dreamed of her that night. Hot, steamy imaginings that had him waking up at dawn grouchy and intensely uncomfortable. The woman was like a fever in his blood. He had to have her, and soon, so he could begin getting over her.

Cassandra was jumpy and irritable all day Saturday. It didn't help that her Medusa teammates had shown up in London the day before to help with the play of Hake El Aran. After her little disappearing act to his yacht last week, her superiors had decided that eyes-on, human surveillance backup was the way to go with this mission. Great. Just what she needed. People watching her every move with the guy. Even if they were her sisters-in-arms and constant comrades for the past two years. It felt like a hell of an invasion of her privacy.

Whoa. Check that. There was nothing private going on or about to go on between her and Hake El Aran.

Vanessa Blake had sent orders along with Monica Fabre, who in her previous life had been a very high-priced call girl, to give Casey any pointers she thought might be useful. Thankfully, the sum total of Monica's advice had been, "You're playing hard-to-get better than I ever could have. In my line of work the point was not to be hard to get. I don't know what to tell you other than keep doing what you're doing. Get the guy panting after you so hard he can't see straight. That's when he'll get careless and let slip with the information we need."

The idea of having Hake panting after her was both intimidating and scintillating. Problem was, she was likely to end up panting after him even worse than he would be after her. And then where would they be? She'd compromise the mission and blow a huge undercover investigation. If it went badly enough, terrorists could end up with the capability to manufacture their own nuclear weapons, for God's sake.

But still. Panting? Every time the thought crossed her mind, she got a little more tense and grouchy.

Some comedian at H.O.T. Watch had sent along a new costume for her with her teammates. She had no idea where they'd gotten it, but the thing was R-rated, pushing X-rated.

Casey unzipped the garment bag in her dressing room, wincing as she did so. The dress really was magnificent. Long-sleeved and floor-length, the gown was black and sheer in its entirety. It came with, in effect, a black bikini and bra for her to wear underneath. The only cover the thing afforded her was a serpent starting at her right shoulder, heavily beaded in tones of copper and gold. It wrapped around her strategically so she didn't look naked. But that was about all that could be said about its body coverage.

Clusters of long, beaded fringe were sewn randomly all over the dress. Whenever she shimmied in it, the entire gown seemed to quiver, the snake alive and flowing sinuously across her body. The costume was entirely gorgeous, and so sexy it embarrassed her to look at, let alone imagine herself wearing.

She was saving it for the late show. Meanwhile, she had to get through the first set. It would be strange dancing with an earbud in her ear. She'd given her teammates strict instructions not to bother her during her performance, however. They were only allowed to talk to her in a life-threatening emergency.

Her microphone pickup was tricky to hide. Belly dancing costumes weren't designed with battery packs and wires in mind. She ended up going with a microsize unit that clipped underneath her right bra strap. It poked her a little bit but was bearable. And thankfully, the unit laid flat enough that it didn't make her costume look weird. She only hoped her perspiration didn't knock the thing out. And she prayed she had no need of it during the course of the evening. Having to call for help at any point tonight would *not* be a good thing.

The hour-long contingency planning session just before she'd come over to the restaurant hadn't helped her nerves one bit. The Medusas had brainstormed everything they could think of that might go wrong during the evening and discussed what the best response to each crisis would be. While she understood the necessity, she really didn't relish talking about what if Hake tried to rape her, or what if he got drunk and passed out in bed with her. Besides, she had no intention of ending up in bed with him, drunk or otherwise.

Of course, her teammates had laughed uproariously when she'd asserted that. She scowled in recollection. Sometimes being part of such a close-knit group was a pain in the butt.

"Ten minutes," the restaurant manager announced through her dressing-room door.

She glanced at her watch. The restaurant had filled up early again tonight. The manager swore it was because people were packing the place to see her dance. She had a hard time crediting that explanation, however. She tilted her chin down and muttered to the microphone in her bra strap, "Is he here?"

"Just walked in," Alex replied. "And may I just say, nicely done, Scorpion."

Casey rolled her eyes. But butterflies were jumping around in her stomach and for some reason, she felt an impulse to check her makeup and hair.

Ten minutes until she would stand in front of him again, half-naked and baring her soul for him. A shiver ran across her skin that was all about anticipating his dark, smoky gaze caressing her and making her feel beautiful. The guy was truly dangerous.

She stretched carefully, going through a quick yoga routine, warming up her muscles and loosening her spine. Appearing boneless was more of a strain on the body than most people guessed. But compliments of her Special Forces training, muscular strength was not a problem. She just had to watch her flexibility. Blood began to flow and her body became warm and limber and supple. She was ready.

Then why was she so jittery and tense?

Because she was about to step out onto a stage and make love to a man in front of three hundred people.

* * *

Hake sucked in a sharp breath as she stepped out onstage. He'd forgotten just how stunning she was. He devoured the sight of her greedily, anticipating having that sinuous sexual intensity all to himself. When she finally opened her eyes after the opening *taksim* dance, she looked straight at him and flashed a private little smile that sent his blood pressure through the roof. Lord, that woman was incredible.

She moved off the stage and out into the audience, momentarily breaking her intimate connection with him. He followed her willowy form, jealously waiting for her to return and dance for him.

"Excuse me. May I sit with you?"

Startled, Hake looked up at the man speaking to him in Arabic. The man threw him a significant look that made Hake start. Here? Now? The contact for the terrorists wanted to talk about the sale of the milling machine? Hake gestured for the man to have a seat.

"You may call me Jabar."

Not a chance in hell that was the guy's real name. Hake nodded. "You already know who I am, of course."

"Of course," the man murmured with an ominous little smile that sent bugs crawling up Hake's spine.

"I'm afraid we're not likely to get much service from the waiters until the show's over or I'd offer you a drink," Hake murmured to the man in Arabic. "The girl's got the staff mesmerized."

"She's not half bad for an infidel whore."

Hake bristled but checked the reaction quickly. He dared not appear sympathetic to anything or anyone western around this man. He studied his guest. The man was perhaps forty-five years old, his body and face starting to sag. Most of his hair was gone, but he had a heavy, black five-o'clock shadow. His eyes...ah, his eyes were sharp. Didn't miss a thing.

Hake glanced up and noticed Cassandra looking at him from across the restaurant. She frowned and her glance slid to the man at his table and back to him, almost as if she were silently asking if everything was okay. He nodded slightly and gave her a little smile. She did an odd thing then, ducking her chin toward her right shoulder and mouthing something. Was that aimed at him or was she speaking to a patron near her, perhaps? He'd probably been looking at her long enough. No sense drawing his companion's attention to her any more than necessary.

He turned back to the man beside him. "I understand we have a mutual acquaintance, Jabar."

"Yes, we do. He passes along his greetings and hopes that everything goes well for you."

"Indeed, it does. My father's company made a significant sale this week and is hard at work preparing to make the delivery. It is always good to have plenty of work to do."

Jabar nodded. "Our friend has also been busy. Although, he has run into a snag in a business dealing of his own. It seems a seller has set an unreasonably high price for a product he very much wishes to procure."

Hake's gaze narrowed. The jerk was here to haggle over the price of the machine? He took a slow sip of his drink and reminded himself that his life rode on not pissing off this man. "In this weak global economy, El Aran Industries has made the decision to take no profit but merely cover the costs of production and paying our workers. My family has enough wealth and does not need more. It is the least we can do to assure our employees remain employed and our customers not only happy but in business."

Jabar leaned forward, studying him intently. "Truly? You sell your goods at cost?"

Hake met the man's eyes squarely. "Absolutely. It is the right thing to do, is it not?"

Jabar pursed his lips. "It is a wise decision. Very wise, indeed. But there is no margin that can be cut at all?"

Hake spread his hands open in apology. "None. I wish there were. But were we to sell our equipment below cost, it would surely attract the attention of government regulators. And we try to avoid upsetting them as much as possible. You understand."

Jabar nodded but didn't look happy. Not the answer he'd wanted. It was a calculated risk not to play ball with this guy's request for a price break. But Hake sensed that any show of weakness now would lead to further exploitation by the terrorists later. Hake did add in a conciliating tone. "When you next see our friend, by all means pass on my family's greetings and best wishes."

Jabar nodded once. If Hake was reading him correctly, the guy seemed to have relaxed fractionally. God willing, their business was concluded and the guy would leave now.

Sure enough, Jabar stood up, disregarding Cassandra, who was moving back toward the stage and about to pass by their table. She pulled up quickly but still brushed into the man. Jabar muttered a rather foul epithet at her in Arabic, which Hake sincerely hoped she didn't understand. As it was, he had to clench his teeth and hang on to his temper not to react to the insult.

Jabar stalked past her and Cassandra moved forward smoothly. As she passed Hake's chair, she murmured, "You all right?"

"Yes. You?" he replied.

She whirled out onto the stage, flourished her finger cymbals, and laughed in his direction. He'd take that as an "I'm fine."

The rest of the show passed in a blur. His thoughts were in turmoil from the visit by Jabar. He second- and third-guessed his refusal to bargain on the price and prayed he hadn't just gotten himself and his family killed. They were, indeed, selling the machine at cost, and he hadn't been lying that discounting the price beyond that would have drawn the attention of all the wrong kinds of people. This deal had to look just like any other deal El Aran Industries did every day.

Whether Cassandra sensed his distraction or not, he didn't know. But he did know she ended her show with a steamy number that she aimed squarely at him, much to the envy of most of the men in the crowd. If her intent was to recapture his full attention, the tactic worked spectacularly.

Casey had barely cleared the kitchen doors before she was on the radio with her teammates.

"Anyone get a picture of the guy who sat down with Hake?"

Roxi answered. "I got one. Sent it to H.O.T. Watch immediately. They haven't ID'd him yet."

"Let me know when they do," Casey replied. She continued, "Did someone follow that man out of here? Something wasn't right about him."

Alex's terse voice answered low, "Cho and I are on him. He left the restaurant, walked about a block east of there and entered the back of a step van parked on a side street. The vehicle has not moved since. Too bad we don't have a full surveillance setup. I'd love to hear the phone conversations emanating from that van right about now."

Monica answered tightly, "I'd like to have an infrared scanner and see what's going on inside that van. I don't like it at all."

Roxi piped up, "Maybe Hake's associate is relaying information to someone and then plans to come back in the restaurant and continue speaking with Hake."

Casey didn't like the sound of any of this. What had that man said to make Hake so tense, and why had the fellow left so abruptly? It had been clear that the guy wasn't happy with whatever Hake had said to him. But Hake had indicated to her that everything was okay. Maybe she was worrying too much about him.

That made her sit up straight and stare at herself in her dressing-room mirror. Since when did she have a personal interest in Hake's well-being? Irritated with herself, she went through her usual between-show ritual of drinking water, eating a tablespoon of peanut butter, repairing her makeup and stretching again.

"Ten minutes, Miss Cassandra," someone called through her door.

"Thank you," she called back. Time to don the risqué serpent gown and blow Hake's mind. She eased the garment over her head and smoothed it down her body. Its weight pulled the gown into a skin-hugging fit against her body. Wow. Nowhere to hide any flaws in this puppy. Thankfully, though, the high neck allowed her to thread a wire around from behind and nestle a microphone unobtrusively just inside the neckline of the gown. Not that she thought anyone would be looking at her neck in this thing.

In sudden inspiration, she reached for her hangers of veils and commenced wrapping three-yard-long lengths of rainbow-colored silk around herself and tucking in the ends to secure them. The traditional dance of the seven veils required the dancer to shed all her veils and end up naked. It was actually a burlesque tradition and not an ancient one belonging to folkloric Middle Eastern dance. But it would serve her purposes tonight. Hake wasn't going to know what had hit him when she was through with him.

She checked in one last time with her teammates. "Any I.D. on Hake's guest?"

"Nope," Alex replied. "No movement at the van either. No telling what the guy's doing in there. Cho moved in closer for a look, but there's a curtain behind the front seat and the back windows are painted over. She spent a few minutes under the van. But other than the fact that it's got a transmission leak, she learned nothing. All was quiet inside it."

Monica asked in alarm, "She's not still under the van, is she?"

Alex replied, "Negative. Cho's back with me."

"Okay, then," Casey replied. "It's about time for my show. Give me a warning if that man heads back to the restaurant even if I'm dancing."

"Worried about your guy?" Monica asked quietly.

"Honestly, yes. I've got a bad feeling about this."

Monica replied reassuringly, "We'll be right here. Roxi, Naraya and I will be at our table, and we've got a clear sight line on the front door. Alex and Cho will keep an eye on Hake's contact. You do your thing and don't worry. We've got you covered."

"And by the way," Naraya murmured, "your first show was wonderful. It's a pleasure to watch you dance."

Coming from a Middle Easterner, that was a fine compliment. Casey murmured, "Thanks. I needed that."

The manager knocked on her door. "It's time, Cassandra."

Time, indeed.

She glided through the darkened restaurant and stepped into the lone spotlight. The audience gasped appreciatively. They knew a veil dance was coming, and she enjoyed dancing for a knowledgeable crowd. She could really cut loose with the difficult, subtle stuff and be assured that they would get it.

The musicians—also not slow on the uptake—shifted immediately into a sexy melody perfect for seduction. She turned her back on Hake and began the slow striptease. Looking at him directly while she did this would have posed two problems: one, she didn't know if she could keep her composure and not lose her nerve; and two, this sort of dance was so provocative she risked embarrassing or offending Hake if she came on to him too strongly in public.

But when she got down to the last veil, a length of black silk wrapped around and around her body, she couldn't resist. She moved over to Hake and offered him the end of the veil. Then, as he held it, she began turning slowly away from him, revealing herself and the magnificent serpent gown to him by inches.

He got a look at the costume before anyone else, and his gaze blazed in response. He looked up at her and the promise was clear in his eyes. He planned to have her and there wasn't a damned thing she could do about it. Her insides quivered in response and anticipation leaped in her heart. Seriously? Was she really that attracted to him? Shock joined the desire zinging through her.

She'd expected a strong reaction from him, but she was blown away by the intensity of his response. Well, all right, then. She'd played with fire. What did she expect? His gaze raked down the costume and back up it again, and she all but moaned aloud.

He nodded slowly. Appreciatively. Possessively. And her knees went weak.

She registered vaguely that the rest of the restaurant was going wild, cheering and whistling and shouting compliments at her in a half-dozen languages. She smiled and held her arms out to them all. But she danced for Hake. He was the one who lit the fire in her belly, the one who made her limbs feel boneless and heavy, who made her breasts ache and her body long for the weight of him.

The result of turning how he made her feel into dance movements was incendiary. Even the musicians grinned and nodded their approval at her as the energy climbed higher and higher in the room. Money poured like water onto the stage and a waiter had to be permanently stationed at the corner of the stage with a push broom to sweep it up. Not that she paid much attention to such things, but thousands of dollars landed on the floor at her feet. Even after she split it with the band, she would have a profitable night. The women's shelter she donated her earnings to was in for a windfall.

"Van's opening," Alex announced in her ear, throwing abrupt cold water on her jubilant mood. "One man emerging. Late twenties. Middle Eastern at a glance. Five foot nine. Medium build. Long black raincoat. Jeans. Black tennis shoes. Heading west."

Crud. That was back toward the restaurant. Casey's smile slipped a notch. She signaled the musicians to slow it down and shift into a folk dance, its traditional movements easy to do. She recruited women from the audience to stand up and dance, freeing her to move around the place. What the heck was going on with Hake's contacts?

"Here he comes," Monica murmured. "Just walked in."

Casey maneuvered so she could spot the guy. No big surprise, he looked around once and then headed straight for Hake. Candlelight from a table he passed illuminated his features. He looked as if he was about to kill someone. His eyes were grim, focused. Dead. She looked down at the guy's coat. It was a warm night out. No need for something that heavy. Unless…

Swearing under her breath, she moved fast, racing toward Hake. She cut across the stage, which gave her an advantage over the young man in the coat because he was forced to wend his way between the tables.

"What's wrong, Scorpion?" Monica bit out.

Casey spotted her three teammates rising, alarmed, from their table in the corner.

She opened her mouth to respond, but just then the man unbuttoned his coat. She saw what was beneath and took a running dive.

"Hake!" she screamed.

Chapter 6

Hake's mind went blank as Cassandra slammed into him, knocking both him and his chair over sideways and rolling him under a table all in one violent movement. They came to a stop just as a second impact hit, this one much bigger, much heavier. It flattened him like an elephant had stepped on him.

Brilliant light, heat, then deafening noise and flying debris, and then the first screams registered. His ears rang. Cassandra's weight was upon him. Her voice yelled urgently. Something about a perp. And a security perimeter. And then she was yelling at him over a cacophony of screams and shouts. "Hake! Are you hurt?"

"I don't think so. What the hell happened?"

"Bomb. C'mon. We've got to go."

"We have to call the police and help the wounded!" he retorted.

"There's no time to be a hero. We have to get you to safety before someone comes back to finish the job!"

"What job?"

"Killing you," she grunted as she pushed off him and into a crouch. "Stay low and stick by me," she yelled over the chaos. Sirens wailed nearby. And then a spray of water, cold and shocking, hit him from overhead. *Fire sprinklers.*

He sat up, looking around in disbelief at the demolished side of the restaurant. The back wall of the stage was obliterated. It looked as if a tornado had struck that one spot. The front of the club was damaged but not destroyed like the area immediately around him. What the hell? A bomb? Why wasn't he blown to bits along with everyone else in here? He opened his mouth to explain that she must be mistaken, but she cut him off urgently.

"Let's *go*." She dragged him to his feet, put her hand on the top of his head and hustled him toward the kitchen.

"The exit's that way—"

She interrupted. "Sniper may be waiting out front to pick you off. We'll use the back door."

She spun into the kitchen low and fast in a move that looked suspiciously military. She waved to him to follow her. And then a tall, elegant blonde woman materialized by his right elbow. He started, but before he could say anything, he became aware of another woman on his left. He lurched in surprise. "Who are you?"

Cassandra looked back impatiently. "They're with me."

With her? What the hell did that mean? He must be in shock because he had a hard time stringing coherent thoughts together. The four women—it turned out there was one behind him, too—all but shoved him through the kitchen, past screaming staff and waiters rushing around grabbing fire extinguishers and heading into the other room. He and his impromptu bodyguards burst out the back door.

The alley was far from quiet with sirens now wailing toward the club in earnest, but it was better than inside. The tall blonde took the lead as they neared the end of the alley. "Wheels this way," she bit out. The woman made some sort of hand signal to Cassandra, who did another hand signal back.

Hake frowned. His security team did stuff like that now and then. And then he was shoved into the back of a minivan, lying on the floor with Cassandra on top of him, while the other women looked out the windows and chattered back and forth about tails and threats and evasive maneuvers.

"Where to, Scorpion?" the blonde called back over her shoulder.

Cassandra replied, "The *Angelique*. The crew will augment our phalanx and it can be moved on short notice. See if H.O.T. Watch can call the captain and tell him to ready the ship to sail immediately."

"Good idea," one of the other women murmured.

What the hell was a hot watch? Hake turned his head, burning his cheek against the nylon carpet, but bringing himself face-to-face with Cassandra. "Who are you?" he demanded.

"Later. We've got to secure you first."

He glared. "Oh, we're definitely going to talk later. And tell the captain of the *Angelique* that Hake wishes him blue skies and fair weather."

"Is that a distress code?" she asked astutely.

He nodded tersely.

"Got that, Mantis?" Cassandra called.

"Affirmative," the blonde replied.

"Mantis? Scorpion? Are you women exterminators or something?" he asked. This whole evening was turning into a surreal nightmare.

"Something like that," Cassandra replied, flashing a wry smile. "Just relax and be patient with us a little while longer."

He commented blankly, "I planned to get horizontal with you tonight, but I didn't imagine it would be like this."

Her gaze snapped to his, wide and startled, vulnerable for a moment. And then she smiled faintly. "That would've been nice."

"The night's not over yet," he murmured back under his breath.

"No, but this is going to be a long one for me. We'll be debriefing till dawn. You, too, I imagine."

"Who do you work for?" he asked in sudden alarm. The deal! The terrorists! He couldn't blow this thing—the entire El Aran clan's safety was at stake!

"All in good time," she murmured soothingly.

"Stop the car. Let me out," he ordered.

She looked at him apologetically. "I'm sorry. I can't."

"You have to! You have no idea what's at stake here!"

"Tell me about it," she asked evenly.

"I can't. Let me out!"

"Hake. My employers need to talk with you."

"No!" he answered forcefully. "I'm not talking to anyone!" In fact, he'd probably already said too much in his panic and disorientation. He closed his mouth and subsided to wait out the ride. Once he was back on the *Angelique*, he'd regain control of this disaster somehow. Make it go away. He could only imagine the favors he was going to have to call in and the strings he was going to have to pull to fix this mess. But he had no choice. *Everything* depended on it.

The van turned a corner and then came to a stop.

"Scorpion, I need an I.D. on these guys," the blonde said sharply from the driver's seat. Cassandra lifted off him, and he registered missing her body pressed against his.

"Those are Hake's men. They're okay."

Hake started at the weapons being brandished around him. "Don't shoot my security team," he snapped. "They cost me a lot of money."

Cassandra held a hand down to him. "We're about to see if they're worth their salaries."

The back door of the van opened and the blonde was there, talking low and urgently with his men, who looked to be in minor shock at whatever the woman was saying. She finished speaking and his men nodded tersely. Then he was dragged out of the van and hustled onto the *Angelique* amid a tangle of weapons and big, tense bodies.

"Where's Cassandra?" he demanded, as he ducked into the salon.

"On the pier," one of his men replied. The guy spoke into the radio clipped to his collar. "We have the principal aboard. Cast off."

"Wait!" Hake ordered. "I want her on board."

"Sir, your security—"

"She knows what happened at the restaurant. And she owes me an explanation."

"But—"

"Do it," he snapped.

The security man nodded and turned on his heel. It was only a few seconds until he heard Cassandra's voice raised in protest. Didn't want to come with him? Avoiding him, was she? Well, that was just too damned bad. Someone had just tried to kill him and he bloody well wanted to know who. Plus, he might need the leverage with her employer to keep him or her from interfering with the sale.

He pushed past the security man blocking the doorway and stared down at her on the dock. He called out grimly, "If your employer wants a single shred of cooperation from me, you're boarding this ship right now, Cassandra."

The group of women glanced at each other in silent communication. And then, reluctantly, Cassandra stepped forward. One of the women grabbed a big duffel bag out of the van and shoved it at her. She took it as she stepped onto the gangplank. Poor girl looked as if she were marching to her own execution. Tough. He wanted answers and he wanted them now.

There was a flurry of activity as his crew stowed the gangplank, cast off and pulled away from the dock. And then one of his men was quietly urging him back inside and safely undercover. Cassandra approached him and he took her firmly by the elbow, steering her inside with him. "You and I need to have a conversation."

She looked at him for just a moment, her expression closed. Stubborn. Didn't want to talk, huh? Not his problem. "Have a seat, Cassandra. Or should I call you Scorpion?"

"I answer to either," she answered evenly.

"What's your real name?" he demanded.

"That's classified."

"Who are you? And those other women with you?"

When she merely shook her head at him, he tried, "Who do you work for?"

"I have to make a phone call. And then maybe I can answer your questions."

He weighed that. Had to ask for permission to tell him anything, did she? "You'll make the call here, where I can hear you."

She nodded and rummaged in her bag for a cell phone.

She dialed a lengthy number. Overseas call, then. "Scorpion here. I need to speak to Viper."

A short pause ensued, and then she began to speak. "I assume you've gotten an initial brief from the team? You know my location? Not surprisingly, he's demanding answers. What am I authorized to tell him?"

Hake waited impatiently as she listened, her expression grim.

"Understood, Viper." She stowed the phone and looked up at him.

"Well?" he demanded.

Casey took a deep breath. How on earth was she supposed to figure out whether or not Hake was in league with terrorists? She couldn't believe Vanessa Blake had told her to use her own best judgment and tell Hake whatever she thought he needed to know based on where his loyalties lay. It was one thing to have her boss trust her in theory, but it was another to be out here on a real-world op where real lives rested on whatever she thought best. Apparently, she'd officially entered the big leagues now.

She ventured a look at Hake. He was not a happy camper, and she couldn't blame him. His mood probably wasn't going to improve when she started interrogating him either. No help for it, though. "So, Hake. Who was that man who sat with you during the first show?"

He looked startled for an instant, but then his face shut down and his gaze narrowed. "Why do you ask?"

"Because it was his compatriot who walked in wearing that bomb vest and tried to blow you to smithereens."

"What?" Hake burst out. "How do you know that?"

"Two of my companions followed the first man out of the restaurant to a van a block from the restaurant. Bomb

Boy came out of the same van, walked up behind you and activated a shape charge at you."

"A shape charge?" he echoed.

She explained, "It's a bomb designed to blow its energy in a narrow, directed cone, rather than just a general area blast."

"I know what a shape charge is," he snapped. "But how do you know?"

She ignored the question. "Why did the first man send a second man to kill you? What did the two of you talk about?"

He ground out, "Tell me who you are."

"Answer my question first," she retorted.

Hake shook his head. It appeared they were at an impasse. A crewman stepped forward to interrupt the Mexican standoff. "What are your orders, sir?"

Hake blinked. "Take me into international waters. And when everything has calmed down, we could use a bite to eat. Whatever's easy for the chef to throw together."

Casey cursed under her breath. If he made it out of English territory, neither she nor the British government would have legal jurisdiction to tell Hake what to do. And clearly, he knew that. Not good. "Look, Hake. You don't trust me, and I'm having trouble trusting you at the moment. So, I'm going to tell you who I am and we'll see if that makes a difference."

He nodded tightly.

If he was in league with terrorists, he might attempt to harm her in the next few seconds. She made sure her cell phone was turned on inside the duffel and her hand resting on a pistol. She took a deep breath and spoke. "My name is Casey—you'll forgive me if I skip the last name for now—and I work for the United States government. We have reason to believe you and your father are doing a business deal with a terrorist entity, and I've been sent here to stop you."

Hake stared at her. His gaze widened in shock and then narrowed in...what was that? Speculation? Irritation? Calculation? She wished she knew him better to read that look.

"You're a spy?" he finally asked.

"Not exactly. Think of me as more of a...soldier."

That made him laugh once, shortly, in disbelief. Not that she cared one way or another if he believed her or not. It didn't make any difference to her mission. The good news was that in response to the revelation, he hadn't ordered his men to lock her up or blow her brains out.

"Okay, your turn," she said expectantly.

He looked at her a long time. A shadow of the desire he'd roused in her back at the restaurant flitted through her mind. She'd never been around a man who could do this to her with a mere look. It bordered on scary.

Eventually, he sighed and said, "My family is being blackmailed into selling a piece of sophisticated manufacturing equipment to an anonymous, but highly suspicious, buyer."

"Do you have any idea who this buyer is?"

"No. That man who sat with me in the restaurant was my first direct contact with the buyers."

"How are the buyers blackmailing you?"

"They've threatened to kill everyone in my family if we don't do the deal. And after tonight's episode, I'm inclined to believe them."

She leaned forward. "Did you refuse to do the deal this evening? Is that why they sent a bomber after you?"

He snorted. "They tried to haggle on the price, but I refused to come down on it. If we did, it would make various governments, including yours, suspicious. Although that is a moot point now, isn't it?"

She frowned sharply. The terrorists must figure the son was expendable and that killing Hake would ensure Papa El Aran's cooperation. She pulled out her cell phone and dialed H.O.T. Watch. Vanessa Blake answered the call.

Casey didn't mince words. "We need to get surveillance and security on Marat El Aran ASAP. The buyer tried to kill Hake to scare Daddy into playing nice. If they can't kill the son, they may go after the father next."

"Got it," Vanessa replied tersely. "How much did you have to tell Hake to get him to cooperate?"

Casey laughed shortly. "I haven't secured that yet. I may have to spill it all, though."

"Don't compromise the Medusa Project," Vanessa warned.

"Understood."

"I leave it in your capable hands, then. Do what you have to. Get the son to help us and find out exactly how much he knows. We'll contact the father as well. Tonight's attack pretty much negated the idea of standing off and waiting for the deal to go down so we can snatch both the terrorists and the El Aran people."

"Hake says the family's being blackmailed into the sale."

"I'll be sure to ask Marat about that."

Casey started. Vanessa was going to lead the team herself? Wow. She only went out on the most crucial and difficult missions in person ever since she'd given birth to her daughter, Caroline, last year.

Vanessa was speaking. "...know where you're sailing?"

"Hake ordered the captain to take us into international waters. I'll let you know when we have a destination."

"Stay in touch."

"Wilco," Casey murmured.

She'd barely disconnected the phone before Hake demanded to know who she'd been talking to. He vibrated with masculine impatience, and something feminine within her thrilled to all that energy. Her reaction was damned annoying, in fact. "That was my boss," she said rather more sourly than his question warranted.

"And?"

She shrugged. "And what? Now you tell me everything you know about these terrorists and my people try to catch them."

Hake shook his head. "Can't risk it. You government types always foul things up and my family will be the ones to pay the price—with their lives. El Aran Industries goes through with this deal as planned and you'll tell your people to stay the hell out of the way."

She considered for a moment, then said, "I hope that's merely your opening gambit, because if it's your final offer, you're about to be very disappointed."

His eyes glittered with anger. Didn't like being threatened, did he? She couldn't blame him. "How's that?" he ground out.

"If you refuse to cooperate with me and my people, you're going to find yourself under arrest, the deal halted and whatever consequences the terrorists threatened coming true against your family."

"You wouldn't," he growled.

She looked him square in the eye and answered low and even, "Try me."

Chapter 7

Casey watched warily as Hake leaped up off the sofa and paced the salon. He reminded her of a seriously riled panther. He snarled, "So that's it, then? I cooperate with you or you throw my entire family to the wolves?"

She took no pleasure in defeating him. Not like this. "Terrorists cannot be allowed to get their hands on that machine. At all costs—including my life, yours and even your family's—the deal must be stopped."

Hake burst out, "My father and I don't want this bunch to have the machine either. We were going to sabotage it so it can't achieve the precision someone would need to fabricate, say, a nuclear trigger."

Casey's eyebrows rose. "Can that be done in a way the buyers can't spot easily?"

Grim humor glinted in his dark gaze. "We expect they'll manufacture faulty parts for six to twelve months before they figure it out. And by then, they'll have burned most of their raw resources."

"Why didn't you contact the British government or your own about all this?"

"Same reason I didn't contact yours. Governments mess things up. They have security leaks and are bogged down with bureaucracy and bungle delicate negotiations."

"We kept you alive tonight, didn't we?"

He stopped pacing abruptly to study her intently. "And you and your friends would be who again?"

"Government agents who are neither prone to security leaks nor bungling delicate negotiations."

"What do you want from me?" he asked directly.

She answered equally directly. "Your full cooperation."

"Not happening," he bit out.

She shrugged. "Nonetheless, my mission remains to stop this deal. I'll succeed with or without your help."

"You can't stop it!" he exclaimed. "My family's lives ride on it going through!"

She sighed. "What if my people were to set up heavy surveillance around the deal to apprehend the buyers?"

"Do I have any say in what you and your people do?"

He sounded bitter. Not that she blamed him. She'd be terribly tense if her family's necks were on the line, too. "No," she answered truthfully. "You don't."

"I can always tell my captain to stay in international water for the next few weeks until the deal is done."

"And throw responsibility for the whole mess onto your father's shoulders?" she said reproachfully. "I think not."

He scowled. She was right and he knew it. He wouldn't leave his father in the lurch like that. She watched in silence as he paced the salon. It turned out he was gorgeous from every angle.

Eventually, he dropped onto the sofa beside her. He asked, "If you hadn't seen that guy and tackled me like that, I'd have been blown to bits, wouldn't I?"

"Probably." They'd been lucky that the restaurant's tables were old and heavy and made of solid wood. That fact alone had likely saved both of their lives.

He reached over and took her hands in his. He looked her directly in the eye. "Thank you," he said simply.

"You're welcome." Their gazes met and touched in a moment of naked honesty. They were *alive.* Such a simple thing but so very precious. He reached up slowly with one hand to touch her cheek, a light touch, just the tips of his fingers trailing across her cheekbone and tracing the line of her jaw. A shiver passed through her, and a single errant thought filled her mind. *Do that again.*

He murmured, "A woman who can dance like you shouldn't also be some sort of superspy."

"Why not?" she murmured back. His gaze was mesmerizing, probing hers with an intelligence that made her worry about how much he was seeing of her.

"It's too much. You're intimidating."

"Me? Intimidating?" She laughed shortly. "You're the intimidating one. All this wealth and success, your perfect looks, brilliant mind, smooth sophistication… I'm just a soldier."

"You have no idea what other people see when they look at you, do you?" he asked, surprised.

"Same thing I see every morning in the mirror," she replied a shade defensively.

"I highly doubt that. I see a beautiful, sensual woman who, for some reason, chooses to pretend to herself that she is neither beautiful nor sensual."

What the heck was she supposed to say in response to something like that? At a loss, she demanded, "And I suppose you don't see movie-star good looks in your mirror every morning?"

He shrugged. "I take no credit for my looks. They're merely the luck of the genetic draw."

She just shook her head. Their worlds were so different that she could hardly imagine his. She suspected he'd be incapable of comprehending hers any better.

Hake startled her by asking, "Now what?"

She replied gently, "Now you tell me everything."

"No, I think this is the part where *you* tell *me* everything. Who are you and who do you work for?"

She sighed. She had to do something to cut the tension between them. Get him to relax and open up to her. It was probably time for some of that pesky boy-girl stuff. If she was lucky, he'd loosen up after nothing more than some pleasant conversation. "I can't tell you anything about me or my employer. It's classified."

"Give me a hint."

"I'm probably the only belly dancer you've ever seen who's been known to pack a Glock 9 mm pistol while she dances."

"You can hide a gun under those skimpy costumes?" She nodded and he laughed in disbelief. "If only I'd known. You'd have been even sexier to watch."

Okay. Time to change the subject. She tried to sound casual when she replied but failed miserably when she croaked, "Tell me something about you I'd never guess."

"I hate the idea of getting married, but my father's trying to force me to do it."

She grinned. "I have no trouble guessing that about you. Tell me something that will surprise me."

"I hate having my picture taken."

"Really? Why would *you* hate pictures? You're gorg—" She broke off.

"Thank you," he murmured in reply to her unfinished compliment. "Being judged for one's looks gets old much faster than you might imagine, however."

"I wouldn't know," she replied.

"Oh, come now," he retorted. "Surely you know how beautiful you are. And just as surely people judge you based on your looks all the time."

"I don't look like this most of the time," she replied drily.

"How do you usually look?"

"Well, I rarely wear makeup. I'm more likely to have mud or camouflage paint all over my face. And I never wear dresses or sparkly clothes."

"I'll look forward to seeing you *au naturel*."

Her gaze snapped to his. Did he mean merely without makeup, or was he referring to seeing her undressed altogether?

He moved on smoothly. "Tell me something surprising about you."

"I used to be a librarian."

His brows lifted. "I confess, I find that hard to picture."

"I was a research librarian, in fact." She omitted the bit about working for the FBI. It had always been her private joke that she was a belly-dancing librarian. She'd never dreamed her longtime hobby would come in handy on a mission. She glanced over at Hake, who was studying her with the kind of focus and intensity that threatened to make a girl feel darned special. She looked away, embarrassed.

"I have twelve sisters," he said unexpectedly.

"Good Lord!" she exclaimed. "My sympathies to you."

He laughed. "I knew a whole lot about girls early because of them. But if you ever tell anyone they used to dress me up like a doll and curl my hair and put makeup on me, I'll deny it to my dying breath."

"Are there pictures?" She laughed. "I'd pay a lot to see those."

"You and a whole bunch of tabloids," he grumbled.

"You don't like being rich and famous very much, do you?" she asked.

"The rich part is admittedly nice. The fame I can do without. But unfortunately in my case, they came as a package."

She nodded in understanding. "Anonymity is critical to my work. I hate public attention of any kind."

"How do you dance in front of crowds, then?"

"I mostly pretend they're not there. Unless someone like you is in the audi—" She broke off, appalled by what she'd just let slip.

He grinned but the expression faded fast. "You won't want to hang out with me for long, then, will you?"

The question startled her. Hang out with him? As in to date him? Good grief. Her mind stumbled hard enough over that concept that it took her a moment to move on to the rest of his comment. He was right. She could in no way afford to come under scrutiny. Reporters would dig into every facet of her life and identity. And although the U.S. military had covered those tracks very well, her lack of a past would raise red flags. Or worse, someone might actually find something on her.

She looked up at Hake and caught his grim look. His features smoothed out immediately and he said lightly, "Well, at least we have tonight."

Alarm exploded inside her. What exactly did he have in mind? She stammered, "Y-you're right. I don't have much time to debrief you. We really need to get busy with that."

"As tempting as it is to make a snappy comment about what you mean by debriefing, I'll refrain," he commented drily. Heat climbed her cheeks tellingly, but thankfully he moved on casually. "I don't know about you, but I'm hungry."

He was stalling. But it was his boat and his crew, and there wasn't a whole heck of a lot she could do to force him to talk if he didn't want to. She sighed. "Fine. Let's eat. And then we'll talk."

He shot her a stubborn look. So, it was going to be like that, was it? She'd just have to do what the Medusas always did. They used brains and creativity to circumvent any situation where they could not resort to brute force. And sometimes they—reluctantly—resorted to girlie stuff. Like flirting with the target over a simple but tasty midnight dinner.

She felt exceedingly weird smiling at him around mouthfuls of croissant sandwich and casting come-hither glances over the cranberry relish. But he seemed to relax as the meal progressed. No matter that she felt uncomfortably squirmy low in her belly and aching for something she had no intention of putting a name to.

It was Hake's turn to dawdle over the meal tonight, avoiding the inevitable conversation to follow, and it amused Casey. After dinner, he moved to stand over by a large bank of picture windows. A stunning view of moonlit English countryside slid past outside.

"It looks like a magical dream," Casey murmured.

"Mmm. An enchanted world," he agreed. "Like you. Too beautiful and elusive to be real."

He was the too-good-to-be-real one. It was hard to wrap her brain around a man like him actually existing. But then Hake touched her elbow, his hand warm and alive and entirely real. He murmured, "I promised myself I would kiss you tonight and, given our mutual brush with death earlier, I'm not inclined to delay much longer lest I never get a chance to do it."

Her stomach and her toes curled into tight knots of anticipation. Her gut warned her in near panic that this was *not* part of the mission. But if kissing Hake would get him to spill his guts, she probably ought to do it…for the good of the mission, of course.

She replied reluctantly, "Kissing is probably not a great idea if we're going to have to work together."

"All the more reason to do it and get it out of the way," he replied in a silky voice that vibrated through her with sexual intensity. "Then we can both relax and quit wondering what it would be like."

"Hake—"

He moved swiftly, drawing her up against him, his mouth swooping down to capture hers before either one of them could come up with any more good reasons not to do it.

Her first reaction was relief. Shockingly, she *was* glad to have the suspended sense of anticipation out of the way. But then…oh, my…a raft of other sensations flooded her. His big, hard body plastered against hers. His warm, wine-flavored lips moving on hers. His hand slipping under her hair, tilting her head to just the right angle.

And then the sheer charisma of the man, all his charm and attractiveness and confidence rolled over her and through her. His thumb toyed with a soft spot just behind her ear as his lips opened her mouth and the kiss grew deeper. More intimate. A hot merlot invasion that was druggingly delicious. His free hand drifted down her back sending electric pulses shooting up and down her spine until she felt hot and boneless all over.

It was a revelation. So much for the theory that she had

no desire to be a girly girl. She was loving every minute of being exactly that in his arms. Worse, she realized her hands had crept over his shoulders and around his neck and that she was pulling his head down to hers as eagerly as he was pulling her to him. This was not happening!

But as sure as she was standing there, her entire body strained forward, pressing into him as if she would become a part of him. She tore her mouth away from his and was appalled to realize she was panting. Hard. Okay, so she'd been lusting after him a whole lot more than she'd admitted to herself. But dang, that man could kiss!

Hake stared down at her, his eyes blazing spots of black fire in the shadows of his elegant face. He looked…shaken. And something warm and satisfied and entirely female unfolded deep inside her at the sight.

"I'm afraid we're going to have to do that again," he murmured.

"But…we can't…" she mumbled.

"Shouldn't and can't are entirely different creatures," he murmured as his mouth closed on hers once more.

Dammit, their second kiss was every bit as incendiary as their first one. More so. Worse, this time he settled into the thing, prepared to draw it out and savor it to the full extent of enjoyment for both of them. She'd never realized two people could kiss with their entire bodies. But as they pressed into one another, hands roaming and breath ragged, every inch of her burned with desire for this man.

He'd temporarily lost his mind. A man like him would never want a woman like her under normal circumstances. But she had to admit, it was a great fantasy while it lasted. Temptation insinuated itself into her consciousness. When in her life was a man like this ever going to kiss her just so again? This was a once-in-a-lifetime opportunity.

And it wasn't as if she was forcing the guy to come on to

her. He was in this purely of his own free will. Of course, he'd also just narrowly missed being blown to bits and was probably half out of his head with shock. She was a bad, bad person for considering taking him up on his offer in his state.

But then he drew her down to the sofa, his hands stripping the shreds of her gown off her shoulders and baring her skin to his mouth. Fireworks exploded inside her head and lower, deep in her abdomen. Oh, yes. She seriously wanted this man.

And then the flawless logic of the hopelessly-in-lust kicked in. They were both adults. If they wanted to have sex, it was nobody's business but theirs, right? They both knew the score. They would scratch the itch and move on like two civilized people.

Except there was nothing civilized in how she felt right now. And she had a sick feeling that he would be hard to move on from. This was the kind of man she could fall for—was falling for. She wasn't as worldly as he was. She hadn't spent most of her adult life jumping in and out of casual affairs flung across the front pages of the tabloids. She'd only had two serious relationships and both of them had ended badly.

But by his own admission, Hake wanted nothing to do with settling down. The fact that his father was pushing him to marry surely made Hake more stubborn on the subject. And why should the guy settle down? Every beautiful, available woman on several continents was throwing herself at him. The man lived in a gourmet candy store. Why should he settle on a plain old chocolate bar like her?

Reluctantly, she pulled away from him. Her entire body felt the loss of his heat and vitality. "I'm sorry, Hake, but this isn't going to work. I'm a Hershey bar, you see."

"Excuse me?" he asked, confused.

"Your life is a Belgian chocolate store with a hundred varieties of gourmet truffle."

His hands slid up her arms, raising goose bumps in their wake and he cupped her face as he drew nearer. "You'll have to explain that to me later. After we've had our fill of each other."

"I can't do this, Hake. Really."

"Because you're a Hershey bar?"

"Exactly."

He stared at her in what looked suspiciously like sexual frustration. "What on earth are you talking about?"

"I'm plain. Simple. I don't do the whole female seductress thing. Exotic, beautiful women of every flavor throw themselves at your feet for the sampling every day. I can't possibly be as captivating or interesting."

"But my favorite brand of chocolate is Hershey."

"You've never had a Hershey bar in your entire privileged life," she accused.

"Hence the novelty and appeal of it, my dear."

She shook her head. "I don't do casual relationships."

He answered lightly, "Then we're in luck. I don't do relationships at all."

That made her pull back sharply. "All the more reason not to do this."

He sighed and shoved a hand through his hair, standing it up all over his head but still managing to look like a picture straight out of an Italian fashion magazine. "I don't know what's happening between us. Hell, I don't even know your last name. But I know I haven't been this intrigued by a woman in...as long as I can remember."

"Chandler."

"I beg your pardon?" he said shortly. Poor guy sounded almost in pain.

"Chandler. That's my last name."

A slow smile unfolded on his face. "See. That wasn't so hard. Chandler. That's a sophisticated-sounding name."

She shrugged, embarrassed by how exposed she suddenly felt. He'd taken away the anonymous soldier persona she'd been hiding behind. "I'm not a sophisticated kind of girl."

He snorted. "You're more complex, and more fascinating I might add, than just about anyone I've ever met. I find you mesmerizing."

"And here I thought it was because you like watching me shimmy around half-naked."

"That, too." He laughed. "You're an extraordinary dancer, by the way."

"Thank you."

They looked at each other for several long, charged seconds.

"Don't do it," she warned.

"How are you planning to stop me?" he asked as he closed the distance between them.

"Well, I could hurt you in about a hundred different ways or just kill you," she murmured.

"But you won't," he murmured back, his hands coming up to cup her face where he'd left off before.

"What makes you so sure?" she muttered.

"Because you like how I make you feel. You want me as much as I want you."

"I do n—"

He pressed light fingers to her lips. "Don't lie to me. I hate it when women lie."

"I hate it when anyone lies," she retorted.

He smiled. "Touché."

They stared at one another, stalemated yet again.

"Help me out here, Hake. I'm going to have to report

to my superiors in the morning, and I've got to have more than you kiss like a god."

He grinned broadly. "A god, huh?"

"Work with me," she all but begged. "Give me something on that man who talked to you in the restaurant. Or better, give me what you've got on the people who approached you and your father."

He stared at her for a long time. She didn't for a minute underestimate how intelligent or calculating a man he was. His personal financial success was ample testament to both.

"Fine," he sighed. "But on one condition."

"What's that?"

"Come to bed with me."

Chapter 8

Hake waited tensely for Casey-Cassandra-Scorpion's answer. He was stunned to admit it, but his desire to make love with this woman only grew the more he got to know her. Who'd have guessed a confident, take-charge soldier lurked under all that organza and beading? An utterly fascinating combination of tough and tender.

"No deal," she said promptly.

"Then I tell you nothing," he retorted just as quickly.

"You don't seem to understand your position, Hake. I could arrest you for obstruction of justice and conspiracy to commit acts of terrorism."

She was hiding behind her soldier persona. He knew women far too well to be snowed by her act, however. He could all but taste the desire dripping off her. "Casey, Casey," he sighed. "Do you know yourself so little?"

"What are you talking about?" she demanded nervously.

He moved slowly, giving her every opportunity to prove him wrong and pull away. But as he'd expected, she did not. A combination of innocence and deadly experience swam in her wary gaze, drawing him to her more powerfully than an aphrodisiac.

"Let me show you," he said. Moving in slow motion, he drew her into his arms. She tensed, and he paused, waiting until she finally relaxed. He kissed his way across her collarbone and up her neck. He couldn't resist a little nibble of her earlobe, but he softened it with whispered word of how beautiful she was. By gradual degrees she went warm and liquid in his arms. The sensation exhilarated him. He wasn't generally fond of seducing innocents, but this woman lit a fire in his blood that was nigh uncontrollable.

Her arms looped around his neck and her body melted like warm chocolate against him. His eyes drifted closed as he savored her lithe curves in his arms.

She said sweetly against his lips, "You have…" a soft kiss "…the right to remain silent…"

He jerked back, startled. "What are you doing?"

"Reading you your rights. It's a required legal procedure in America. I don't know if we're still in British waters or not, so I went with my own country's recitation of legal rights while I arrest you."

"By what authority?"

"By mine. I'm a commissioned military officer, and as such, I have the right to arrest you. If you'll turn around and place your hands behind your back while I get out my handcuffs…"

Stunned, he stared at her. She didn't sound the slightest bit playful about that handcuff offer. "What the hell—" he started.

"I'm not joking, Hake. You're under arrest."

"And then what?"

"Then I'm commandeering your vessel and ordering the captain to go back to London so you can be put in jail."

"You can't!"

"I am."

Sonofa— For the second time tonight, he felt completely disoriented. First, someone tried to blow him up, and now this. She actually planned to arrest him! It wasn't his fault those people had approached him and tried to force him to sell them a precision milling machine. And it wasn't his fault they'd tried to kill him. None of this was fair.

"Why am I the bad guy all of a sudden?" he demanded. "I've done nothing wrong. I'm not a terrorist."

"But you are obstructing an investigation of terrorists. And that's a felony."

He rolled his eyes. "I'm trying to protect my family."

"Fine. Then go to jail and protect them all you like from there." She added grimly, "If you can."

He scowled at her, supremely frustrated.

"Or," she continued implacably, "you can let me help you. I have resources at my disposal you've never dreamed of. And contrary to your opinion, my team has never failed on a mission."

"There's a first time for everything, and I can't afford for this to be yours to fail," he snapped.

She stared at him with something akin to sorrow in her gaze. "Do you seriously think these terrorists will let your family live even if you do sell them the milling machine? They'll blackmail the El Arans until you don't have anything else they want, and then they'll kill you all. Your family is dead men—and women—walking. Particularly after you had the gall to live through tonight's attempt to kill you. You've embarrassed them."

"So by saving my life tonight, you killed us all?" he asked incredulously.

She shook her head. "Your family is rich, powerful, connected to governments and to the global business community. You represent everything they hate. They were already planning to come after your family."

He sat down heavily on the sofa, swearing under his breath. She was right. Horror rolled through him as he absorbed that truth. He looked up at her bleakly. "What do you need from me?"

She sat down beside him and said simply, "Tell me everything."

"And you'll tell me everything in return? Let me participate in all operations?" A stubborn look flickered through her eyes and he added desperately, "They're my family, for God's sake."

She sighed. Nodded. "All right. But promise me if I ever give you a direct order you'll follow it instantly and without question."

That sent his eyebrows up.

She added, "You're a civilian. I'm a trained Special Forces operative. I need to know you'll do what I tell you to if you're about to die."

Special Forces? Her? His mind locked up in disbelief. Surely not. Although she certainly had the nerves of steel down cold. Yet again, this woman had knocked him completely off balance. He nodded shortly. "Deal."

"Start at the beginning," she urged gently.

He sighed and began talking. She listened intently, without interruption. At the end of his recitation she asked a million questions and typed copious notes on a laptop computer that emerged from her duffel bag. Finally, an eternity later, she hit several buttons and nodded in satisfaction.

"Done," she announced.

"What is?"

"My report to my headquarters. They'll sift through everything you gave me and no doubt will have a bunch of questions of their own. But we've probably got a few hours to catch a nap before they contact me."

He felt like a washcloth that had been wrung out and hung up to dry. He also felt unexpectedly lonely. And vulnerable. Perhaps it had taken this long for the reality of how close he'd come to dying earlier to sink in. And for the reality that his family was in just as much danger to hit him.

"What are your people going to do to protect my family?" he asked.

"Your family already has an extensive personal security team, does it not?"

"We do, but it didn't do me a bit of good at the restaurant."

"You also didn't have your guards with you. I have faith you won't make that mistake again anytime soon. I'm sure by now my people have been in contact with your father and made it clear to him that no El Aran is to set foot outside without a full contingent of bodyguards. It would be best for your family to sequester itself somewhere safe, like your family's compound in Bhoukar, until this operation is concluded."

He felt slightly better, but his gut still rumbled warningly at the idea of his family's lives depending on agents of any government.

She changed subjects abruptly. "This milling machine you're selling the terrorists is big and heavy, I assume?"

He snorted. "It weighs several tons. We'll need a crane to lift it."

She commented thoughtfully, "They'll likely want to move it by ship, then."

"You're planning to give them the machine?" he asked, surprised.

"If we can't catch them by any other means, we'll have to go through with the deal. We'll use your suggestion and sabotage the thing. And, of course, we'll put tracking devices on it—" She broke off abruptly, a look of dismay crossing her face.

"What?" he asked sharply.

"Has your crew swept this vessel for tracking devices recently?" she asked tightly.

"I have no idea."

"Ask. Now."

He leaned over and pressed the intercom button. "Captain Soderling, have you checked the *Angelique* recently for tracking devices put here by someone interested in following us?"

"Not in the past week, sir," a deep voice answered in alarm. "Do you have reason to believe there is such a device aboard?"

Casey leaned forward to speak and Hake pressed the button for her. "Captain, as soon as it's feasible for you to do so, I need you to have your men comb every inch of this ship. You'll need to drop anchor, deploy divers and inspect the hull as well. And if you find a device, *don't* disable it. Is that understood?"

"Mr. El Aran?" the captain asked. Hake grinned. The man didn't know what to make of one of the boss's female guests giving orders. Especially an order like that.

"Do as the lady says, Jürgen."

"Roger, sir. I'll wake the crew and get started on it right away."

As the ship halted and men commenced crawling over it from stem to stern, Hake put in a ship-to-shore call to his father to make sure the El Arans had been warned.

Casey spent the time typing her personal report detailing the night's activities for her superiors.

Hake never did get through to his father. He left urgent messages at every contact number he had and then prayed the reason the phones weren't being answered was because the El Aran security team had already gone into lockdown. When the worry became too much for him, he broke down and asked Casey, "Do your people have some sort of status report on my family? Are they safe?"

She looked up from her computer surprised. "I'll ask." She made a quick call while he fretted. In a matter of seconds, she smiled reassuringly at him. "They're fine. The whole clan has gathered at your palace in Bhoukar and is under heavy security."

He sagged, relieved.

"Do you really live in a palace?" she asked.

"No. I live in a flat in London. But the family seat could probably be called a palace without exaggerating."

She just shook her head.

The ship's crew made their way through the salon just then, tearing the place completely apart before putting it back together again. As they moved on to other parts of the ship, Hake asked Casey ruefully, "Do you cause this much chaos everywhere you go?"

She smiled wearily. "On most missions, we slip in, do our thing and slip out without anyone ever knowing we were there. In a perfect world we're quiet and invisible. So, no. This is not a typical mission."

"Who is we?" he asked curiously. "I was not aware that your country had more than one belly-dancing commando in its service."

She laughed. "When you put it that way, it does sound a little strange, doesn't it?"

He frowned. She was smoothly ducking the question. "Who are you?" he persisted.

"I can't answer that. My unit is highly classified."

"I told you everything. I think I've earned a little information back—"

"Sir!" One of the crewmen burst into the salon. "We found it!"

Hake leaped to his feet quickly, but Casey beat him off the sofa. "Show us," he demanded.

The two of them followed the sailor down to the yacht's engine compartment. In the very rear of the vessel where the propeller screw exited to the water was a small metal object that looked like a radio transmitter. Casey examined it and then announced, "GPS unit. They can track us anywhere in the world."

"Shall we remove it?" the sailor asked.

She shook her head. "Not yet. And keep looking. They probably have more than one device aboard. I would if I were them."

Hake was amused by the incredulous looks his men threw her way when she wasn't looking. He knew the feeling. She appeared so soft and harmless but spoke like a trained killer. The woman could really quit knocking him off his feet like this. He didn't know what to expect from her next.

And sure enough, she surprised him when she spoke again. "It's nearly daylight. Why don't you lie down and try to get a little sleep, Hake? Once my superiors start working you over, you may not get another chance to rest for a while."

The ship's security chief, a Swiss fellow named Tomas, piped up. "And you would be who, ma'am?"

She smiled pleasantly at the man. "I'm not at liberty to divulge that information."

"Do you work with that woman on the dock? The one who told me how to do my job?"

Hake watched with interest as Casey fielded that minor grenade. "You'll have to forgive my teammate if she stepped on your toes. We'd just pulled Hake out of a bombing and were tense about getting him undercover. My colleague didn't know who you were and I'd had no chance to brief her. She only wanted to make sure Mr. El Aran was safe, same as you."

Tomas looked mostly mollified, particularly when Casey added, "Maybe later this morning we could discuss your ideas on where we should stash Hake to maximize your security team's effectiveness."

"Hey!" Hake objected. "I'm not getting stashed anywhere. I'm participating in whatever happens!"

Casey and Tomas traded downright friendly looks of commiseration with one another. The crew continued searching the ship, and Hake showed Casey to the lower deck staterooms, which had already been searched.

Hake paused in the narrow passage. "Do you want your own room, or for security reasons, would you like to be closer to me?"

She looked up at him, worry momentarily winking in her gaze. Afraid to bunk in with him, was she? Smart girl. But then amusement flared in his gut. She'd thrown herself in front of bomb and bullied him into cooperating without batting an eyelash. But sleeping with him scared her? He added lightly with just a hint of a dare in his voice, "You can take the bed. I'll take the couch."

"You'll do no such thing," she declared. "You sleep and I'll stand guard."

He snorted. "There's no way I'm going to sleep if you're hovering over me like some protective, UZI-toting mother hen."

She retorted drily, "I don't like shooting UZIs. They climb too much when you go full automatic with them."

He just shook his head and opened the door to his suite for her. He was shocked when she actually stepped inside ahead of him. A frisson of pleasure skated over his skin. She was going to stay with him, then, was she? Starting just inside the door, she worked her way counterclockwise around the luxurious space, examining it minutely from floor to ceiling. "What are you doing?" he asked.

"It's called a security sweep. I'm looking for listening devices, cameras and hiding places for possible assailants."

"This is a yacht. Every inch is used carefully. Space for bad guys to hide in is extremely limited."

"Nonetheless, I'm personally searching your room."

He waited patiently until she finished her sweep. "So, are you brave enough to sleep in the same bed with me?" He pointedly left out any promises to behave himself.

Her gaze narrowed. "Is that a challenge?"

He grinned. "If that's what it takes to get you in my bed, absolutely."

"In that case, I accept."

Chapter 9

Casey watched apprehensively as Hake disappeared into the bathroom. She might talk a good line, but inside her head a voice was screaming a big, fat, what-the-hell-are-you-doing at her. She was mature enough not to have to accept every stupid dare someone flung at her. And sleeping with Hake was definitely stupid. Thrilling, but stupid. Apparently, being a sensible Hershey bar didn't necessarily equate to making sensible decisions.

The bathroom door opened and Hake emerged wearing a pair of silk pajama bottoms—and nothing else. His bare chest, bronze and perfect, made her gulp. Any number of reactions to the sight came to her mind, most of which ran along the lines of *hubba hubba*. He was much larger and more muscular than a person noticed at first with him. His tailored suits and sheer charisma had a way of distracting a person from the size and raw power of the man.

"There are towels, toothbrushes, shampoo and robes

in the bathroom," he said, gesturing over his shoulder. "I think there's skin-care stuff and some cosmetics, too."

She'd bet. It was probably standard procedure on this vessel to be prepared for female guests sorely lacking in luggage or toiletries. As Hake threw back the covers and started to climb into bed, she fled for the bathroom.

She scrubbed off the remnants of her stage makeup and studied herself in the mirror. Seeing her like this would be the end of Hake's infatuation with her. The soldier was fully revealed now that the glamorous dancer's mask was gone. Oh, well. She'd warned him. He would see her as she really was as soon as she stepped through that door.

Funny, but part of her was reluctant to break the spell of her Cassandra persona between them. Had she actually been enjoying pretending to be beautiful and exotic and desirable? What on earth was wrong with her? She hadn't worn makeup in something like two years before this mission came along. She lived in combat boots and fatigues, often filthy and nearly always toting lethal weapons, which she had used on more than one occasion, thank you very much.

As regret ignored her arguments and stabbed at her anyway, she insisted to herself it was for the best this way. She had a mission to do, and she held no illusions that working with Hake would be easy. He was smart, stubborn and used to being in charge. Kind of like her, in fact, which was exactly why he was bound to drive her crazy.

She sighed and pulled on the tank top and skimpy shorts she found folded neatly on the bathroom counter. Discretion being the better part of valor, she left her bra on under the top. Thus girded to step back into battle with Hake, she opened the bathroom door.

The lights were off and the stateroom was pitch-black. Good thing she'd already memorized its layout. She made her way to the far side of the bed and slipped beneath a fluffy down comforter. The stupidity of agreeing to get into bed with a lady killer like Hake struck her full-force, and she went as stiff as a board.

"Are you all right?" His voice floated out of the inky darkness close by.

"Why do you ask?" she gritted out.

"It feels like you're on the verge of bolting."

"I am not."

He asked mildly, "Tell me, Casey. Why did you panic when I kissed you before?"

"I didn't panic!"

"Then why did you feel obliged to interrupt an inspired kiss, if I do say so myself, by trying to arrest me?"

"I was doing my job."

The bed shifted, and it felt as if he might have turned to face her and propped himself up on an elbow. He said gently, "You were hiding behind your job. Are you that afraid of being the woman you are?"

The words jolted through her like lightning, singeing her from head to toe. Was she afraid of being a woman? Was that why she hid behind combat boots and rifles? Most of her teammates still went out on dates, still did their hair and put on makeup and sexy little dresses during their off hours. But not her. She was the job. Always the job.

She must have been quiet for too long because he murmured, "Come here."

"Why?" she asked cautiously.

"It'll be easier if I show you." A hand touched her hip and she jumped about a foot straight up in the air. Lord, she was tense.

He murmured easily enough, "I won't do anything you don't want. Say the word and I'll stop. You have my word of honor." His hand shifted to her elbow and he drew her lightly toward him. She tried to brace herself, but the boat was rocking slightly and chose that particular moment to roll toward him. She overbalanced and threw out her hands to catch herself. Acres of warm skin sprang up under her palms and she gasped in surprise.

Hake gave a tug on her wrists, pulling them out from under her, and she fell on top of him unceremoniously. "Sorry," she grunted. "Just being a klutz."

He fell silent for a moment, then asked reflectively, "Why are you so tense about having sex with me?"

"I'm tense about *not* having sex with you," she snapped.

His voice, rich with amusement, tickled her ear. "There's no need to worry about it not happening. It will."

"That's not what I meant—" She broke off. He knew that; he was teasing her. "You're incorrigible."

"Mmm. I've heard that before." His lips touched her temple lightly and she about jumped out of her skin. "What's the problem, Casey? Why not sit back, relax and let things unfold naturally between us?"

"Nothing's unfolding here."

His fingertips traced her shoulders lightly. "Would it be so terrible if something did?"

"It's just…wrong."

"What's wrong about making each other feel good? Exploring the attraction between us—and don't try to deny that it exists. I've been playing this game too long not to know sparks when I see them." She remained stubbornly silent and he continued. "You're a consenting adult, as am I. You're sensuous and passionate. Why not savor both? Here we are together and alone. We're even already in bed and half-undressed. All you'd have to do is let down your guard and it would be right there for us to enjoy."

He must be a deadly negotiator to sit across a conference table from. "It's not that simple," she replied stubbornly.

He relaxed beneath her, which she somehow found even more threatening than if he had continued to push his case. "What's not simple about this, Casey?"

He was asking for it. She took a deep breath and fired both barrels at him. "This may be simple for you. See a chick you want to bed. You go after her, get the prize and move on to the next attractive female who comes along. That's fine for you, but it's not how I operate. I want the real deal. A relationship and feelings and long-term commitment." She hesitated but then forced herself to press on. "I happen to be attracted to you, Hake, which means I want more—and won't settle for less than—an actual relationship."

He chuckled beneath her. "Here we go. The lady's thrown a set of conditions on the table. Let's negotiate and close this deal, then. What constitutes a relationship in your mind?"

She frowned. "Spending time together. Sharing personal stuff. Having feelings for each other."

"I'd say we've started doing all of those already," he replied. "Now all we have to do is sustain them."

"Ah, but here's the kicker," she added grimly. "There has to be a possibility of more." That would stop him in his tracks for sure.

"As in, say, marriage?" he asked. Abruptly all humor was absent from his voice.

Ha. That had gotten to him. But as the idea of marriage rose before her and thoroughly alarmed her, she surprised herself by being the first to temporize. "Well, a long-term commitment, if not actual marriage."

His voice floated out of the dark. "I think I can agree to that."

She froze, stunned. "I beg your pardon?"

"My father has decreed that I must marry within a year. I currently have no serious wifely prospects in mind, but as of this week, I'm officially open to the idea, like it or not."

"What about true love?" she asked, aghast. "Finding your soul mate?"

He shrugged, his chest moving against hers in a way that completely distracted her for a moment. She felt the turbulence of his thoughts, but he declined to answer. "What will you do?" she asked in a hush.

"I love my family. And if I haven't found my soul mate after all the women I've dated, I highly doubt I'm going to now. I will search for the least objectionable candidate I can find and marry her."

"I'm sorry," she whispered. She couldn't imagine what it must be like to be forced into something so important and personal by an outsider.

His hand smoothed over her hair. "You're kind to worry about me," he murmured. "But I don't deserve your concern. I really am a cad when it comes to women. I'm probably way overdue for a comeuppance."

"I don't know about that. You've been completely honest and forthright with me. And not every man affords women that courtesy."

"Don't try to make a hero out of me, Casey. You're the hero here. I'm the useless playboy."

She lifted up on her elbows to frown down at him. "The way I hear it, you've been spectacularly successful in your own right."

"In business, perhaps. In love, not so much."

"Why's that?" she asked. "What inside you is keeping you from loving someone?"

"I haven't a clue," he answered soberly. "Care to take a stab at it?"

She answered thoughtfully, "My guess is you're afraid that women will love your wealth and fame and not *you*. I think you're secretly a romantic and don't want to get your heart broken, so you hold all women at arm's length emotionally."

"That's some theory you've got there," he mumbled.

"Does it ring true deep in your gut?" she pressed. If only she could see his face. She leaned across him and reached out, fumbling for the lamp on the nightstand.

"What are you doing?" he demanded.

"I want to see your face when you answer so I can read whether or not you're lying." The light flicked on and they both squinted in its glare. She stared down at him expectantly. "So, am I right?"

He exhaled hard. "Maybe."

Oh, yeah. He might be having trouble admitting it to himself, but all the signs were there. Who'd have guessed the big, bad playboy was such a softie inside? She spoke quietly, "I think you'll do fine with marriage. Just let your wife see this side of you and you'll find happiness."

He snorted. "And where am I going to find a woman I can trust with these feelings?"

"You mean besides me?" she commented wryly.

His gaze snapped to hers. As she watched, his eyes widened and then darkened. Alarm started buzzing in her own gut. "What?" she finally asked as he continued to stare at her.

"You are a woman, aren't you?" he asked, apparently speaking mostly to himself.

She laughed. "Last time I checked."

"I'm serious," he retorted.

"So am I."

Reluctant humor shone in his gaze. "You certainly can give back anything I dish at you, can't you?"

She blinked down at him, not sure what he meant. "I guess so. It kind of comes with the territory when you're a woman working in a male-dominated world."

He shook his head in what looked like disbelief. "A belly-dancing commando. Who'd have guessed you'd turn out to be so wise?"

Right. As if her life was a shining example of smart decisions, particularly when it came to love. Casey made a face. "I may be a lot of things, but I highly doubt wise is one of them."

His fingers traced a line across her shoulder and under the hair at the back of her neck while his thumb caressed her neck lightly. "You underestimate yourself. I think you're a rather brilliant Hershey bar."

She laughed, and maybe that was why she was surprised when his lips touched hers. Her humor evaporated in a nanosecond, leaving her equal parts shocked and nervous. What was happening between them?

But then, even that fled her mind as his mouth moved across hers. She'd never heard of a man tasting so good— dark like coffee, with a bite like whiskey, but sweet as well, like vanilla. She sipped of him to her heart's content, and he was generous, opening himself to her explorations and not rushing her. His teeth were smooth and even, his lips firm and warm. And his tongue was ever so clever, dancing lightly with hers.

His hands were not idle while they kissed, stroking along the undersides of her arms and down her ribs to her hips, raising goose bumps from her hairline to the tips of her toes. Eventually, she tore her mouth away from his and pushed herself up to a sitting position, straddling his waist with her thighs. She had to get control of this situation. Of herself.

Except, somehow, she wasn't in control at all. His hands trailed lightly down her body starting at her neck, down the valley between her breasts and across her belly. She shivered, craving more. A sound of need escaped her, stunning her. She had no memory of consciously making a decision about him, but apparently she had.

"You know my condition, right?" she murmured.

He nodded solemnly. "I can't promise you happily ever after, but I will give you everything I'm capable of in the meantime."

Was it enough for her? A real relationship...for a little while at least. It was as risky as heck. She was bound to get hurt, but the ride promised to be spectacular right up to the moment it crashed and burned. Hake was patient beneath her, waiting still and silent for her to wrestle it through. And that was probably what tipped the scales.

"This is insane," she mumbled.

"Indubitably." A dazzling smile lit his face. "Welcome to the asylum."

She just shook her head. But inside, the little voice in the back of her head was doing back flips of excited anticipation. She was really going to jump off the cliff and fly with Hake!

Getting their clothes off took a little maneuvering, but in a moment, Hake settled her back on top of him astride his hips, naked as the day she was born. He seemed in no hurry to proceed and merely looked at her, a slow smile spreading across his face.

"You're beautiful," he murmured.

It was hard for her to accept the compliment, especially from him, but she made herself let the words flow through her until she had absorbed them. "Thank you. You're pretty beautiful yourself."

He smiled as he reached up to tuck a strand of her hair behind her ear. "Come here, Casey. Let me show you just how beautiful you are to me."

She leaned forward until their mouths met. He reached out to turn off the light, and the last thing she saw before darkness enveloped them was Hake's gaze glowing with appreciation. Their joining was achingly slow and entirely perfect.

As the sensations piled one on top of another, each more delicious than the last, her body undulated in rhythm with the rocking of the boat beneath them. The twin movements amplified one another until everything was a tangle of limbs, a slide of hot skin on hot skin, a flurry of urgent kisses and gasped words of pleasure.

Hake surged over her, giving himself entirely to her and she to him. They rode the wave together until it crashed around them with an explosion behind her eyelids that all but rendered her blind and deaf. She cried out and Hake's hoarse cry mingled with hers as they surrendered to it together.

He rolled to his back and she collapsed on his shoulder, spent. His chest rose and fell hard, and perspiration slicked his skin against hers. He still smelled of coffee and whiskey and vanilla, but now a new note was added to the bouquet. Startled, she recognized her white orchid perfume on his skin.

A force moved within her, shifting and expanding before settling into a new place, deep in her heart. She liked the smell of herself on him. A lot. Nearly as much as she liked the feel of her body on his. Or her mouth on his. Or her hands on him.

His voice came out of the dark. "Thank you. I've never received a gift to compare."

"You probably say that to all your—"

He forestalled her, pressing a finger to her lips, as if he would protect the specialness of the moment. She subsided, letting the silence of it wash over her. They *had* shared something special.

But how special?

Special enough to hold his attention for a long time to come?

She forced the doubts out of her mind. There would be time enough tomorrow for regrets and recriminations. For tonight, it was enough to know she'd touched him as deeply as he'd touched her.

When she emerged from his shower the next morning, steamed to perfection, she was alarmed to see Hake talking on her cell phone.

"Ah, here she is," he said. "It was a pleasure speaking with you, Vanessa."

Casey's eyebrows shot up. He was already on a first-name basis with her boss? In minor shock, she took the cell phone he held out to her. "Hi, boss. I gather you met Hake."

Vanessa laughed. "Sounds like you're going to have your hands full with him. Good work talking him into cooperating with us. After I spoke with his father, I was skeptical of your chances. Marat seems to think his son is more than a little willful."

"That's a word for him," Casey replied drily.

"We got your message about the tracking devices. We concur with you—leave them in place. But in the meantime, we've got a problem. Rumors of Hake's death are rattling the European banking community. The British prime minister has asked the president of the United States to have us reveal that Hake is alive so there's not a nasty shock on the London Stock Exchange."

"But that'll expose him to the terrorists!" Casey protested.

Vanessa sighed. "I know. The good news is I think we can make lemonade out of this particular lemon."

"How's that?"

"If we have to show Hake anyway, why not use him as bait to draw out the terrorists? If we flaunt him loudly enough, they'll be honor-bound to make another try at him. I'll need you to work with his security team to protect him while we taunt the hostiles into showing themselves."

Casey winced. On the one hand, she loved the idea of getting to spend more time with Hake. But on the other hand, she purely hated the notion of using him as bait. "Have you decided when and where you want to put on this dog and pony show?" she asked in resignation.

Casey listened carefully as Vanessa described what had been arranged for them. Her boss finished with, "Got all that?"

"Yes, ma'am. We'll be ready."

"I'll relay the necessary instructions to Captain Soderling," Vanessa replied. "Get some rest. You're going to have a busy day tomorrow."

Now that was an understatement. She disconnected the call thoughtfully.

"What's up?" Hake asked from beside her.

"You and I are going on a little trip tonight."

"Oh, really? Where?"

Protocol dictated not upsetting the protectee. Except it felt weird not telling Hake everything. She knew it had been a bad idea to get involved with him! One night and already duty and obligation were clashing. She dodged carefully. "We've got a few hours to rest while my boss makes the arrangements. I'll fill you in once the details are finalized."

He studied her intently. "If I threaten to torture it out of you, will you tell me what's going on?"

She grinned down at him as he lounged beside her. "You can make all the threats you like, but you can't take me in a fight."

"You think not?" he asked. "When this is all over, we'll have to give it a go. I wrestled at Cambridge, you know."

"Let me know if you need me to lose intentionally to save your fragile ego."

"Don't you dare," he retorted, laughing.

"All right," she said mildly. "But I warned you."

He chuckled.

"What?" she demanded.

"You are completely unlike any other woman I've ever known."

"Is that good or bad?" The question was out of her mouth before she could suck it back behind her teeth.

He grinned widely. "I'll let you know when I've reached a verdict."

She stuck out her tongue, and he pulled her down to him. Their lips met. As their kiss spiraled out of control and it became clear that breakfast would have to wait for a while, Vanessa's parting words echoed in her ears. "Casey, stay out of trouble."

Right. No problem. A boy and girl thrown together in a life-threatening situation…tons of stress in need of burning off…a fancy yacht and a world-class playboy who kissed like a god…it all spelled *Trouble* with a capital *T*.

Chapter 10

Hake stared at Casey across the breakfast table. "Your government sent a bunch of *women* to Bhoukar to protect my family? Do you know *nothing* about my country?"

She smiled tightly. "Actually, we know quite a bit about it. We've run several successful missions in Bhoukar. In fact, we have a standing offer of both hospitality and military assistance from the emir any time we're in that part of the world."

His country's dyed-in-the-wool traditionalist leader supported a group of women soldiers? Hake felt his jaw sagging. "So, what's the plan?"

"We'll use the tracking devices on this ship to mislead the terrorists into believing we're sailing up the Irish coast. But meanwhile, you and I will head elsewhere. When we're in place, we'll spring the trap. With you as bait, of course."

"Of course." Hake sounded grim. Smart man.

She met his gaze equally grimly. "I don't like it any more than you do. Maybe less. But I've got direct orders from my superiors, and the stakes are huge. My hands are tied." She smiled lamely at him. "If everything goes well, we'll nab your terrorists and they'll never bother you or your family again."

"And if things don't go well?"

"Then people will die."

He shuddered at how matter-of-factly she said that. "Have you ever killed anyone?"

"Yes," she answered shortly, looking at a spot over his shoulder.

"How many?"

She made eye contact with him then. Her gaze was closed tight. "Do you seriously want me to answer that question?"

"Good point. Never mind." He sipped his coffee while he considered her. This was a first. He'd never been with a woman who was a killer. He probably should run screaming from her. But damned if she didn't fascinate him.

"Why do you do what you do?" he asked curiously.

She answered without hesitation, "Because I get satisfaction from knowing I'm making a real difference."

"You like your work, then?"

"I love it."

He nodded in understanding. He was passionate about his work, too, managing the El Aran financial empire. He loved the thrill of billion-dollar bets, outsmarting the next analyst, beating the odds. "How long do you plan to do this job?"

She pushed scrambled eggs around her plate thoughtfully. "As long as they'll have me or until I die."

That startled him. "Is mortality high in your line of work?"

"We've had a few close calls, but my team hasn't lost anyone." She added reluctantly, "Yet."

He nodded in commiseration. "In my world, deaths are inevitable, too."

Her lips twitched. "Banking is dangerous stuff, huh?"

"No. Being a jet-setting wild child is dangerous."

She commented under her breath, "You don't seem like much of a child to me."

He reached over to place his hand over hers. "Thanks. I generally prefer grown-up toys." He felt the shiver that passed through her. Such a responsive woman. "How long do you think this fishing expedition to draw out the bad guys will take?"

She shrugged. "It will depend on the terrorists and how fast they move in response to seeing you alive. A few days. Maybe a week."

One week with her. That wasn't long. Was it long enough to know if she was The One? Long enough to make a life-changing decision about the two of them? How in the hell was he supposed to figure that out in one lousy week?

"When will you know what our destination is?" he asked.

"I knew that last night. I just wanted you to get some decent rest before I made you all tense again."

That sent his eyebrows upward. A woman who could keep a secret? The surprises just kept on coming. "So, where are we going?"

"The French Riviera."

"You are aware that paparazzi crawl all over the Gold Coast, right? Because of my…notoriety…we won't be able to breathe without them on top of us."

"I believe that's the idea," Casey replied. "But never fear, your men and I will keep you safe—"

"You expect to be with me in a security capacity?" he interrupted.

"Yes."

"No, no. That won't do at all," he declared.

She stared at him. "Excuse me?"

"I don't need you as my bodyguard. I need you as my girlfriend."

"Come again?" she blurted.

"You heard me. If you're going to be with me, you have to be my girlfriend."

"You have a reputation for never doing relationships. It'll make the terrorists suspicious."

He shrugged. "I doubt they've studied my social habits that closely. And besides, think of the rumors it'll start. The press will go crazy if they think the most eligible bachelor in Europe is about to be landed."

That was definitely dismay on Casey's face.

He frowned. "You're the one who wanted a real relationship. Why the cold feet going public with it?"

She mumbled absently, "I have to make a call."

He watched, bemused, as she pulled out her cell phone.

"Vanessa. He wants to drag me around with him in front of the press as his girlfriend. They're going to want to know who I am. They'll dig—"

Ah. She was worried about her privacy. He snorted. She had no idea the invasion of it she was about to endure. He was loathe to warn her, though, lest she think better of being involved with him at all.

Casey said tightly into her phone, "You'll send me the dossier when it's built?" She hung up the phone after a murmured goodbye.

"What was that all about?" he asked.

"I can't exactly have the press digging into my life."

"Why? Are you an ax murderer?"

"No. After this mission I need to be able to disappear again and not be some sort of celebrity."

The idea of her disappearing from his life sent faint waves of nausea rolling through him. He didn't want to lose her. At least not like that, with no trace, as if she'd never been here. A week. He had one week to change their future.

Chapter 11

Casey grabbed onto the railing at her back as the big helicopter established a hover overhead. The French Puma helicopter was too big to land on the yacht's helipad, but they needed the big bird's extended range and lifting capability to get them to their destination.

"Are you sure this is going to work?" Hake shouted in her ear.

She grinned over at him. "I've done this a hundred times. Just remember what I said and do what I showed you."

"I know, I know. Keep my weight close to the rope and don't let go."

"When you get to the door, let the guy in the 'copter do all the work and maneuver you inside. Your job is to make like a sack of potatoes for him."

Hake nodded as a big, metal seat lowered toward them on a steel cable. His security chief, Tomas, rode up first. The seat came down again. "Your turn!" Casey shouted.

Hake threw her a devil-may-care smile that made her knees wobble and climbed onto the seat with effortless grace and power. She gave a thumbs up to the PJ hanging out the helicopter door on a harness, and in a rush of wind and salt spray, Hake was away.

It felt uncomfortable not being at his side, as if an umbilical cord between them was being stretched too far. The seat slithered back down toward her too fast. She jumped out of the way and steadied the heavy seat without bothering to scowl up at the PJ overhead. Men always tried to mess with the Medusas the first time they worked with the female Special Forces soldiers.

She climbed on the seat efficiently and gave a thumbs-up. As she'd expected, the PJ ran the hoist full-speed, yanking her into the air alarmingly fast. When she jerked to a stop beside the door, she waved off the PJ's hand, grabbed the hoist arm overhead and swung her feet up and out, flinging herself neatly into the helicopter's cargo bay and landing in a crouch.

She glanced over her shoulder at the gaping PJ and casually called him a less-than-polite name in flawless French. His sagging jaw turned into a grudging grin.

Tomas's men came up the hoist, followed by their gear. The helicopter's nose dipped and they sped away from the *Angelique,* leaving the vessel's sleek silhouette behind in the dark. The yacht would sail up the coast of Ireland, carrying its load of GPS tracking devices, and hopefully the suspicions of the terrorists, with it.

The working theory was the bigger the shock when the terrorists realized Hake was not only alive but flaunting that fact, the better the odds of infuriating them into attacking. Hence, the secret evacuation from the *Angelique.*

Hake was grinning and loving the ride strapped in the back of the big helicopter. As for her, she figured it was some sort of Pavlovian reflex to sleep in choppers because she was either heading into a tough mission or coming home exhausted from one. Her eyes drifted closed and she fell asleep in a matter of moments.

A kick on her foot jerked her back to consciousness some time later. The ocean had been replaced by dark farmland below the helicopter. And they were at low altitude and slowing down. They must be at Calais. She couldn't see the train station from this side of the bird, but it would be out there.

Sure enough, a few seconds later the helicopter's forward speed slowed to zero and a black hole of a landing pad came into sight below. The bird thudded to the ground and the scream of the engines cut off. Casey jumped out first and turned to steady Hake, but he didn't need the help. The man was as agile as a cat. He grinned at her as they jogged out from under the rotor blades and rounded the tail of the helicopter.

A long, sleek shape waited on the train tracks in front of them. The TGV, *Train à Grande Vitesse*. Also known as the French bullet train.

"We're headed for the last car," she murmured. "The one with all the window shades pulled and the lights off."

"Sounds romantic," Hake murmured. When she rolled her eyes, he amended. "You have to admit, it's very sexy and super-spyish to have a car on the TGV all to ourselves to sneak aboard and ride in secret."

She smiled widely at him. "What can I say? I have the world's best job."

Tomas and his men had formed a tight phalanx around her and Hake. As a group they ran to the train and piled aboard fast and quiet. Within thirty seconds of entering the train car, Casey thought she felt it ease into motion. She lifted the edge of a shade enough to verify that they were moving. Okay, that was cool. The TGV had been waiting just for them.

"How long will it take us to get to Nice?" Hake asked.

"Seven hours," Casey replied. "There's a private sleeping compartment at the back of the car. You might want to get some rest. It'll be morning when we get to Nice and Vanessa scheduled a press conference for you at the hotel shortly after we arrive."

"Efficient, isn't she?" Hake grumbled.

Casey smiled. "That's us. We waste no time getting to the point."

"Oh, I don't know about that," he drawled. "You took your time last night...to good effect, I might add."

And in a single sentence, the air between them was thick and charged with sexual vibes that hung as heavy as jungle vines. His gaze smoldered. "Come with me?" he murmured. She glanced doubtfully at Tomas and his men and Hake added, "They may as well get used to seeing you be my girlfriend now. We'll be going public soon enough."

His *girlfriend*. The word rattled through her, unfamiliar and thrilling, and hard to fathom.

"Please? I sleep better with a woman in my arms."

She laughed. "Now that's a great pickup line."

"But it's true."

"Oh, I believe you. That's what makes it such a great line."

As darkness enclosed them in the tiny compartment, Hake seemed to fill the entire space. It was odd and thrilling feeling so small and relatively weak around anyone. He stripped her clothes off by feel and she returned the favor, loving the texture of his body beneath her hands.

The bed was already folded down, and he laid her upon it gently. He stretched out beside her, and she did, indeed, cuddle up to him, more comfortable than anyone had a right to be. His chest rose and fell slowly beneath her ear and she reveled in being with him. They might not have forever, or even have long, but they had now. And now was pretty nice.

The train was nearly as smooth and powerful as Hake's lovemaking as the miles flew past. Eventually, they collapsed in each other's arms, sated and exhausted, and slept. When Hake finally shifted beneath her as dawn peeked around the window shades, she smiled up at him sleepily and was warmed to her toes by the easy smile he gave her back.

Tomas startled her by calling from the other side of the door, "We'll be arriving in approximately ten minutes, sir. Miss Casey's colleague, Vanessa, has confirmed that your hotel suite is ready. A limousine is waiting for us at the train station and French Special Forces will be driving the vehicle. They are also performing a security sweep of your accommodations as we speak."

"Thank you," Hake called back.

"My people didn't arrange for the limo or the security sweep," Casey muttered, alarmed.

Hake kissed the end of her nose lightly. "The El Aran name is not without a certain influence. I suspect my father made calls to a few friends in the French government."

Sometimes she forgot the guy was practically Bhoukari royalty. "Right. Well, I'd better freshen up a bit if I'm to look even vaguely worthy to be seen on your arm."

He laughed as she climbed out of the narrow bed. "No one will ever mistake you for arm fluff, my dear."

"Drat. I guess I'll have to try harder, then."

He grinned. "I can't wait to see this."

She made a face at him as she reached for her makeup

bag. She emerged from the tiny private bathroom just as the train was pulling into the station.

It was a strange sensation letting Tomas and his men sweep her along in their midst as if she was the one being protected. They were tall enough that she couldn't see a darned thing past them, which made her jumpy. A black limousine loomed in front of them and someone put a hand on her head to guide her inside.

Familiar, strong arms gathered her close in the dark interior. "There's my girl," Hake murmured.

She snuggled close to him with a sigh of pleasure. The ride to the hotel, a posh beachside resort, was all too short. They pulled into an underground loading dock and took a back elevator up to their penthouse suite, completely out of sight of the public. The message light was blinking on the phone in the living room when they arrived. Hake took the message and then passed the receiver to her. "It's for you."

Casey sat down beside him to listen to the message from Vanessa Blake, who ran through their schedule for the day—the press conference and then various television interviews with major news networks for most of the afternoon to talk to Hake about his close call with death. Vanessa ended with, "I'll leave tonight's itinerary to Hake to arrange. Far be it from me to tell the master how to play wildly and visibly. Oh, and Hornet arranged a little gift for you to help with the mission."

She glanced over at Hake. "Did you hear the bit about tonight?"

He grinned. "Aye, aye, captain. Wild and visible it is. Who's Hornet, by the way?"

"Roxi. She's the fashion stylist who helped me develop the Cassandra look."

"The woman is a goddess. Although she had an exquisite canvas to paint upon."

Casey smiled skeptically. "Careful or you'll give me a fat head."

"All women deserve to be spoiled a little. Good romance is in the details."

And apparently he had every last detail down to a fine science. One of Tomas's men came in to announce that the hotel laundry was steaming Hake's suit for the press conference. It would be back in ten minutes, and breakfast was on its way up.

Wow. They'd only been here a grand total of about two minutes. She asked Hake curiously, "Do all hotels race around trying to anticipate your every whim like this?"

He glanced up from the *London Times* the guard had handed him. "I suppose they do. I don't pay much attention to it."

She snorted. Why should he, when everything ran like a well-oiled machine around him, and his smallest need was met before he even knew he had it?

He rose to his feet and offered a hand down to her. "Breakfast, my dear?"

He read the financial sections of a half-dozen newspapers over the meal while she glanced through the world news. He ran once through the prepared statement H.O.T. Watch had worked up for him and faxed to the hotel.

"Do you need me to fire some practice questions at you to get you ready for the media?" Casey offered.

Hake grinned. "No, thanks. I deal with the worst elements of the press on a daily basis. Nothing these guys can throw at me will trip me up."

She wished she was that confident. After breakfast she

went into her bedroom to check out Roxi's gift. She didn't see anything out of the ordinary, other than an incredibly elegant room that she could never dream of affording on her own. She peeked in the bathroom—nothing. And then she opened the closet. The row of garment bags sent a thrill of delight down her spine. Oh, Lord. She was turning into a girly girl by the second.

Each bag had an index card pinned to it with instructions on when to wear it, how to accessorize the outfit and even instructions for what lingerie each required. She grinned. Roxi knew her too well.

She found a bag labeled "Press Conference." It held a gray, pin-striped suit that was nice, but looked about four sizes too small for her. Frowning, she took it into the bathroom and tried it on. The jacket turned out to be a cute, cropped cut and the skirt—what there was of it—was a mini that, along with the four-inch stilettos in the bag, made her legs look a mile long. Casey twisted her hair up into a loose French knot and secured it with the crystal-encrusted barrette that had been provided for the purpose. There were even hose and hoop earrings in the bag. The diagram of how to apply her makeup and what shades to wear in front of television cameras might have been insulting if she didn't know what a perfectionist Roxi was. Laughing, Casey pulled out her cell phone and dialed her teammate.

Roxi didn't bother to say hello but burst out, "Do you love it?"

"How could I not? Thanks, Rox. How did you arrange all this?"

"The hotel's concierge hooked me up with a local personal shopper. She took pictures of clothes in the stores and sent them to me, and I told her what to buy. Did she leave you instructions for everything? I told her you were totally fashion-challenged."

"I'm not that bad. I can do my own stage makeup now."

"Yes, but if you did that for daytime wear, you'd look like a very scary clown."

"Maybe you'd better fly down here and keep an eye on me, Mom."

Roxi laughed. "We'll be joining you in a day or two. Vanessa wants us to run standoff surveillance on you and your hunky boyfriend."

Casey winced. Yup, the gig would be up the moment her teammates watched her and Hake together. She lied and said, "I'll look forward to having you guys close by for support."

"Just be careful until we get there. These are seriously bad dudes we're messing with. You were lucky in London."

Thus sobered, Casey hung up the phone and stepped out into the living room. Hake glanced up from a faxed document and did a gratifying double take. He held out the papers and someone took them out of his hand as he strode over to her. He took both of her hands in his. "You look fantastic."

"You look pretty snazzy yourself," she replied shyly. His tailored suit lay across his shoulders without a single crease, the starched shirt pristine, the silk tie perfectly knotted.

"It's time for us to go, sir," Tomas announced.

Hake held out his arm to her with a smile. "Shall we?"

She slipped her hand into the crook of his elbow. "We shall."

Tomas and his men escorted them into a ballroom with

a stage set up across one end of it. Lights already blazed as reporters made preliminary reports. A buzz went up and all eyes—and cameras—turned on Hake.

Casey jolted. "Holy cow."

Hake murmured back, "This is nothing. Wait till a horde of paparazzi turns on us."

"Hoo yeah," she muttered.

Hake was as smooth and polished in front of the press as any politician. He read the statement expressing his condolences for those injured in the London bombing, thanked the local law enforcement, fire and medical crews who had responded to the incident and promised to do all he could to help the British government find and bring to justice those responsible for the bombing.

The questions, predictably, focused on how Hake had gotten out of the nightclub unharmed and where he'd been since. Casey was impressed at how adroitly he dodged the questions. As he'd promised, no mention of any female commandos was made. And then the question they'd all been waiting for came out of the crowd. A reporter shouted, "What do you plan to do now, Mr. El Aran?"

Hake turned toward the voice and fired off one of his patented bad-boy grins. "I nearly died in that blast. Now I plan to celebrate being alive as hard as I possibly can."

"Who's the girl?" another reporter shouted.

Hake blandly ignored the question as Vanessa and company had suggested. The more mystery surrounding Casey, the more media frenzy would be whipped up. She could only pray the cover story H.O.T. Watch had put in place for her would hold up to scrutiny.

Hake thanked the journalists and stepped down off the stage. Tomas had strategically placed her at the foot of the steps leading off the dais, and Hake headed straight for her. He dropped a kiss on her startled mouth. As he turned her loose, he murmured, "No turning back now. It's you and me, together all the way."

The two of them together? All the way? She liked the sound of that a whole lot more than she wanted to admit. And to think. The fun was just getting started. She gulped. What on God's green earth had she gotten herself into?

Chapter 12

Hake knew just the place. The French Riviera was known for its nightclubs, but one discotheque stood out from all the rest when it came to wild parties and high-end clientele: The Grotto. It was possible to get to the place by water and walk down its private pier to the club. Or there was the newcomer's traditional way of arriving. Seeing as he and Casey were supposed to be making a splash, he chose the latter.

As they stepped out of the limo in front of the sleepy little bar, Tomas looked at him questioningly. Hake muttered, "I wouldn't want to deprive her of the full experience."

Tomas shrugged. "It's your funeral, sir."

Casey glanced back and forth between them suspiciously. Hake ushered her into the dim joint. It was narrow and deep and crowded with bistro tables. She frowned up at him. "I thought we were going to a hopping nightclub."

He grinned back. "We're there."

Her frown deepened. "What's the joke?"

"No joke. Come with me." He couldn't keep a grin from playing at the corners of his mouth as he led her to the back of the club. "We have to separate for a moment, I'm afraid. If you'll step into the ladies' restroom, I'll head into the men's room with Tomas and the boys. We'll meet you after that."

As she stared in confusion, he swept into the men's room with his bodyguards. "Hurry, Tomas," Hake muttered. "I want to beat her downstairs."

"She's going to kill you," Tomas muttered back.

Hake grinned. "That's the beauty of it. She can't. She's under strict orders to act madly infatuated with me."

"I'm not saving you from her when you get back to the hotel. That woman scares me. And besides, you'll deserve it...sir."

Hake grinned at his guard and stepped over to the fire pole mounted in the corner. He slid through the hole in the floor and dropped easily onto the red velvet sofa below. A bell rang and a crowd of partiers applauded him as he sprawled on the cushions. He had to roll aside fast, though, because Tomas and his men weren't about to leave Hake unattended for long. Hake regained his feet, straightened his clothes, and turned to wait for Casey to join him on the pole from the ladies' room.

He should have known that landing in an unceremonious heap on a couch was not Casey's idea of a grand entrance. Her feet appeared through the gap in the ceiling. The bartender commenced ringing his bell to announce her arrival. Casey's red stiletto heels alone were naughty enough to set a guy's heart pounding.

Slowly, she twirled down the pole. Her shapely calves came into sight, then her knees and thighs. Her dress slid nearly up to her hips, and the crowd whistled and cat-called as she spun down, her legs gripping the pole in a way that made a man break out in a sweat.

She let go with one hand and leaned back, exposing her throat to everyone and nearly exposing her breasts as her low-cut dress pulled tight across her swelling chest. Eyes closed and a look of sexual ecstasy on her face, she slid slowly down the last dozen inches. The club drew a collective breath of appreciation, and then the place went wild.

She landed on her feet like the sofa was her own personal throne and held an imperious hand out to Hake. Grinning, he stepped forward and steadied her as she stepped down regally.

"Nice entrance," he murmured under the din. "In case I haven't mentioned it recently, your legs are perfect. In fact, all of you is just about perfect."

Her mouth smiled flirtatiously, but her eyes glinted an amused dare at him. "What next? Are we supposed to have a big fight and tear each other's clothes off by way of making up or something?"

He laughed. "Although that would undoubtedly land us on the pages of the tabloids, I think your spectacular entrance rather took care of that. Let's circulate a bit and make sure to run into, and then snub, all the undercover gossip columnists. They know I hate being splashed across the gossip rags, so if I tick them off, they should have a field day."

"You know who all these undercover reporters are?"

"If I told you a crazed terrorist was in this room, could you find him?"

She blinked. "I expect I could. It is my job, after all."

"There you have it. Spotting reporters is my field of expertise."

"Fair enough." She smiled bravely. "Lead on."

Oh, how he did want to lead her on. But not here. Not like this. She was the kind of woman who deserved better than being publicly flaunted like a cheap prize—or a very expensive one as the case might be. An image of his married sisters, safe in their homes with doting husbands, flashed through his head. Hake stopped cold, stunned.

The last thing he wanted was a traditional Bhoukari marriage with a traditional Bhoukari woman. But all of a sudden, he comprehended the concept of privacy in a relationship as a good thing. Not that he'd ever bothered to provide it for a woman before. He lived a fast, visible life, and any woman who wanted to be with him could deal with it.

Then why did he want to take off his suit coat and put it around Casey's shoulders? To gather her protectively close and take her someplace quiet where they could be alone... even if it was only to talk? Why were his teeth gnashing at the idea of every other male in this place ogling her like a piece of meat?

"I'm sorry, Casey," he murmured.

She threw him a perplexed look, but the dance music cranked up painfully loud just then, and they were swept along with the crowd out into the middle of the dance floor.

This was one place he didn't have to worry about Casey handling herself. The woman simply knew how to translate music to movement. Envious looks flew his way fast and furious from the men, and jealous looks from the female patrons shot Casey's way.

At one point he leaned forward to shout in her ear, "Having fun?"

"Yes! It's nice not to have to worry about giving everyone else a good show."

At least one of them was having fun. Maybe it was the

business of waiting for someone to try to kill him again that had him on edge. Or maybe it was his grossly mistaken expectation of being amused when the other men circled his woman like a pack of sharks. But tonight, he found himself clenching his jaw a lot and exhibiting an unusual tendency to touch Casey's arm or rest a hand on her back as they moved on and off the dance floor.

Long after he was ready to take a break from dancing and wet his throat, Casey finally nodded to him. He led her into the next room, which was ringed by a long bar and dotted with sofas.

"You've killed me, woman," Hake declared.

She laughed. "What we just did is not a fraction as strenuous as Middle Eastern dance. Are you admitting, then, that belly dancers are buff?"

"I concede the point." He toasted her with a bottle of water.

They chatted as best they could over the blaring music. At around midnight, the DJ thankfully backed down on the volume, and Casey was able to ask reasonably normally, "Why'd he turn down the noise attack?"

"The patrons need to start working their pickup lines," Hake answered in amusement.

"Seriously?" Casey asked in surprise, looking around.

"Yes."

"So. Is it customary for you to hit on the women or do they hit on you?"

He blinked at the frank question. "I suppose it's more of a mutual thing. I see a beautiful woman, she sees me. We meet, we talk, we—" He didn't know how to finish that sentence tastefully.

"Go back to your place for hot sex?" Casey supplied drily.

"When you put it like that, it sounds cheap. Boring."

"How would you put it?" she asked.

He stared at her for a stunned moment. "Now that I think about it, I suppose the whole business is rather cheap and boring."

Her eyebrows went up. She seemed almost as surprised as he felt. Since when was he tired of the playboy life?

Casey commented quietly, "I'm sorry to be cramping your style like this."

"On the contrary. You're enhancing my reputation spectacularly."

"And what, exactly, is that reputation?"

He leaned close and murmured, "I always go home with the most beautiful woman in the place."

Casey turned a critical eye on the rest of the club. "I don't know about that. The blonde in the corner is stunning. Maybe we should go set you up with her. Or maybe you prefer a more exotic look. Like that African woman—the tall, slender one with the incredible eyes. Or—"

"I'm already with the most beautiful woman in the place," he interrupted gently.

She shook her head. "I don't think so."

Hake captured Casey's ice-cold fingers to keep her from bolting from him. He asked, "What's going on? Are you panicking on me?"

She mumbled, "What do you mean?"

"I came with you. I'm leaving with you. Unless, of course, you want me to go flirt with one of those other women so you can get into a catfight and hit the tabloids that way."

"I'd accidentally kill someone. I'm not accustomed to holding back when I fight."

Hake laughed. "Duly noted."

Casey spoke in a businesslike fashion. "Okay, I've dirty

danced for you. And now you're holding my hand. What's next?"

"You don't have to sound like I'm about to extract your tooth with pliers. The idea is to relax. Have fun."

"No, the idea is to draw attention to you. To get your… friends…to show themselves."

He sighed. She'd lost the spirit of fun from earlier, apparently. She was going to hide behind the whole playing-soldier thing unless… Inspired, he murmured, "It's time for you to crawl onto my lap."

"I beg your pardon?" Casey looked alarmed.

"You need to drape yourself all over me. Imagine yourself tipsy, bordering on drunk enough to lose all inhibition. Trust me. It's how these transactions are conducted."

Reluctance in her eyes was replaced by grim deter-mination. Didn't like mauling him in public, did she? They were in agreement on that score, then. Nonetheless, she leaned across him, ostensibly to set her drink on the end table beyond his elbow. And when she was physically draped across him, she glanced up. The sidelong look she gave him was so incendiary that he felt his clothing and various body parts catching on fire.

"Okay, I'm draped," she murmured. "Now what?"

"Uh—" he cleared his throat "—now we should probably kiss."

She leaned forward until her mouth was barely an inch from his. "Like this?" she whispered.

"Uh, yes. Exactly." And then her luscious mouth was on his, moving coaxingly, as if she thought he needed encouragement to go crazy for her. Her head tilted and she kissed him more aggressively. Her body pulsed forward, her chest coming up hard against his, her arm going around his neck wantonly.

Lights exploded inside his head and shock vibrated

through him. This was more than lust. More than man-sees-woman, man-wants-woman. This dug deep into his gut. Soul deep. The difference between a little buzz and a hopeless addiction. She flowed over him and through him like the finest wine, warm and spicy and complex.

Thankfully, she eventually came up gasping for air because he had no power to do so himself. He blinked, surprised to find himself in a dance club with people and noise and lights around him. Tomas was grinning like a Cheshire cat.

"Did I get it right?" Casey murmured low.

He laughed shortly. "If you got it much more right, you'd have killed me."

She smiled and slid coyly off his lap. If Casey wasn't an old pro at this game, she was, at a minimum, a hell of an actress. She fit into the party scene as if she was born to it. Meanwhile, he felt out of his depth. What in the hell had she done to him?

He was *still* flummoxed when, about an hour later, she leaned in close and murmured, "The patrons are starting to hook up. They'll be leaving soon. If you and I are going to make a grand exit, now's the time, while we still have a good audience."

His gut clenched. He ought to kiss her again. But he was suddenly terrified of doing so. What if that other kiss hadn't been temporary insanity? What if he was losing himself to her?

What was this? The great ladies' man, Hake El Aran, afraid? Of a simple kiss? Bah. He'd kissed so many women over the years he couldn't even begin to guess how many. Some of them had been pretty spectacular kissers, too. Casey had just surprised him. He hadn't expected her to throw herself into that earlier kiss with quite so much unbridled enthusiasm.

He leaned forward cautiously. She was just a woman. It would be just a kiss.

He drew her across his body to prove to himself that he could do so without losing control. Except as her softness and heat molded to him, he couldn't help relishing the sensation. He swore under his breath. Apparently, she was a fix of heroin and he an overdue junkie after all.

One kiss. And then he'd let her go.

Except when his lips touched hers, everything else evaporated, leaving only them in this magical place of pleasure and unslaked need. She tasted like coconut and rum—sweet and spicy. Dammit, she was as addictive as he remembered. It *hadn't* been his imagination! He speared his hands into her thick, silky hair and shamelessly drank from her, feeding on the taste and scent of her until his head spun madly. And then she all but ate him alive.

He couldn't think about anything but getting that dress off her and pulling her down on top of him while he plunged into her. His hand slipped under one of the garment's thin spaghetti straps while his other hand climbed her thigh, sliding under the hem of the slinky little dress. Ah, yes. Silken flesh. About to be naked and joined with him. His woman. Need to possess her pounded through him.

A throat cleared nearby. "Uh, boss?"

Hake tore his mouth away from Casey's long enough to glare at Tomas. He was about to turn back to making love to her when a bright mirror flash got in his eye. He swore to himself. He was in a nightclub. A very public nightclub. With an avid audience watching him and Casey all but devour each other.

Violent impulses ripped through him. "Later," he managed to grit out at her from between his clenched teeth. "When we're alone." He forced his hand to push the shoulder strap of her dress back up and smoothed her hem down her thigh before, through sheer dint of will, making himself set her aside.

He was not the kind of man who fell on any woman like a wild animal. Ever. But he literally shook with the effort of restraining himself. He put his hand on the small of her back and guided her toward the seaside exit. "Get us out of here," he managed to order Tomas.

The chilly night air cleared his head a little, and the long walk down the pier to the powerful speedboat his men had waiting made him feel a little more sane. But not much. Why was he so freaked out? They were already together. He'd even promised her he might consider marrying her. Was he really that big a commitment-phobe? Or was it something else? Was he developing *real* feelings for a woman? Was that what was messing with his head so badly?

No doubt about it. He'd lost his mind tonight. To a seductress sweeter than honey, hotter than fire and more mysterious than the rarest burgundy.

"Let's go back to the hotel, shall we, darling?" he murmured.

"Uh-huh." She sounded drugged, or perhaps so lost in lust she could hardly see straight. He felt a tiny bit better knowing he was not the only one so afflicted.

In a few minutes, they reached their hotel's pier. When they arrived at the penthouse, she kicked off her high heels and joined Tomas's men in sweeping the suite. It was disconcerting how quickly she shifted from sexy girlfriend to all-business soldier.

His head spun and he couldn't seem to clear it. He'd had very little to drink—he'd been far too busy enjoying Casey. It was one thing to talk hypothetically to her about a permanent relationship, but it was another thing entirely to see it starting to develop.

"Are you tired?" she murmured under her breath to him.

"Need to think," he mumbled. "You must be tired… Let you rest… See you in the morning…" He headed for the master bedroom, vaguely aware of Casey staring at him as he stumbled to his room. Someone closed the door behind him, and his bodyguards looked back and forth between him and the closed portal in amazement.

Frankly, he was pretty damned amazed himself. He couldn't remember the last time he'd had strong enough feelings for a woman to forgo sex in the name of honoring both her and those feelings.

Casey leaned against the closed door of her bedroom, unsure whether to sob in heartbreak or scream in fury. *One night.* That was his idea of a long-term relationship? One lousy night? Well, okay, one night, one train ride and one sexy date. Big diff.

And to think she'd been letting down her guard with him for real in the club, exploring her feminine side and discovering to her great shock that she enjoyed flirting with the right man.

She ought to be thanking her lucky stars that the jerk had dumped her this fast and hard before she really got emotionally invested in him. Right? Then why did she feel as if her stomach had just been used as a punching bag?

She stripped off her clingy little dress, threw on sweat pants and a sloppy T-shirt, scrubbed off her makeup and crawled into bed. And waited for relief from the grief and desire ricocheting through her body like out-of-control bullets.

She couldn't possibly have more than an infatuation for Hake after such a short time. This would pass in a day or two. It was just lust. A crush. None of this was real.

One thing she knew for sure: Hake El Aran had no idea

whatsoever of how to have a real relationship. She felt sorry for whoever his father forced him to marry. The poor girl was in for a miserable and loveless life.

As for her, she wanted more.

At least she hadn't made too huge a fool of herself in front of Hake's bodyguards. Sure she'd crawled all over Hake in the club, but they all knew that was just part of the act. The last thing she needed to do was have a torrid affair with Hake El Aran in front of his men. Word would get back to the Special Forces community in a heartbeat, and she would never hear the end of it. Yup. She'd dodged a bullet tonight.

Then why did she feel as if a bullet had torn right through the middle of her heart?

Chapter 13

Grumpy and tired the next morning, Casey dressed for exercise. She needed to do something physical and violent. Sleep—or a notable lack of it—had made two things clear to her. She'd definitely cared more for Hake than she'd realized. And just as definitely, she'd narrowly avoided destroying her reputation and career.

In that same vein, as satisfying as it would be to tear out Hake's eyeballs, she had a job to do. Terrorists to catch. She had to suck up her personal hurt feelings and go on with the mission. But from here on out, it would damned well be on her terms. Girding herself to face Hake, she stepped out of her room.

He had his nose buried in a newspaper and said little to her over breakfast, which was just fine with her. She ate a light meal, and then turned to Tomas. "So, am I going down to the gym to work out, or can you and your guys make me break a sweat?"

The bodyguards grinned as one. Tomas, dressed in jeans and a polo shirt, replied, "Thought you'd never ask. Full contact or just to the touch?"

She laughed. "What's the point if it's not full contact?"

Hake's newspaper came down. "What are you talking about?"

She answered breezily, "Nothing. Go back to your stock quotes."

The guards were already pushing the furniture out of the middle of the living room. "Street rules?" Tomas asked eagerly.

She nodded and stepped into the clear space. The Swiss man stepped forward and the two of them circled each other for a few moments, assessing one another. Then he lunged. She slipped to the side and dropped him like a rock with a blow to the back of the head as he charged past. It was classic Medusa strategy. Don't try to overpower a stronger opponent. Just don't be there when he attacked.

The other men stared. Tomas got up slowly, shaking his head. "I knew you'd be fast, but not that fast."

"Try again?" she asked him.

He nodded and settled into a fighting stance once more. This time he was cautious, focusing his efforts on wrapping his arms around her. It was a good tactic. Why chase her if he could make her stand still? But it still took him nearly ten minutes of grappling and lunging to finally subdue her. "Uncle," she announced good-naturedly from within a crushing bear hug.

Tomas grunted, "This is only a stalemate. As soon as I turn you loose, you'll be back at full strength. And in the meantime, I can't do anything else because it's taking all my energy to restrain you."

"If you had a partner you'd be okay," she pointed out.

"Still, that means I'd have to use two men to take you

out." Tomas turned her loose and she leaped to her feet and whipped around to face him all in one movement. He was ready for the attack, though, and mostly fended off the rain of blows she loosed on him.

"Hey!" Hake called sharply. "We've got places to go and be seen. Don't give the girlfriend a black eye!"

Tomas stopped fighting instantly, and it was only by dint of her excellent reflexes that she stopped her fist from plowing into the man's nose and breaking it. She turned to Hake, who scowled. She'd never seen him look that mad before, not even when he'd learned that terrorists had tried to kill him.

She answered tartly, "If I did get a black eye, you could always tell the paprazzi that you and I got carried away with rough sex. It would do wonders for your reputation as a bad boy."

His scowl deepened even more. He bit out angrily, "I don't hit women."

She took the towel one of the men offered her, wiping her face as she strolled over to him. "Good for you. I'd hate to have to break you in half."

He glared at her. "You know, it's not the slightest bit attractive to say things like that to a man."

She draped the towel over her shoulder. "Where is it written that women have to be wilting lilies to be attractive? Why should I pretend not to be strong and able to take care of myself so a man like you can feel macho and protective?"

He stared at her. "Don't you want a man to take care of you?"

She stared back. And then laughed shortly. "I can take care of myself."

"Then what's a man good for in your world?"

Maybe it was because he'd taken her by surprise, or

maybe it was because he'd pissed her off with his brush-off, or maybe it was because a tiny part of her did like the idea of a big, strong man looking out for her that she snapped, "In my experience, men are only good for one thing." She waggled her eyebrows suggestively, then continued, "And barring that, they're only good for decoration."

Hake stared at her in open shock. Apparently, having his philosophy about women thrown back in his face was like having a bucket of ice water dumped over his head. She snorted. That was just too darned bad.

She turned on her heel and marched into her room to take a shower. Only after spending a good long time under the soothing jets could she admit to herself that men—some men, at any rate—were good for other things. When they weren't being insecure about the girl doing too dangerous and manly a job, that was. Did the other Medusas get that from their men, or was it just her? Was she really a man-hater at heart? She'd never thought so, but now she wondered. Was *she* the problem?

Maybe love just wasn't in the cards for her. The idea of falling in love with someone else at the same time they happened to fall in love back was a minor miracle. Throw in a whacky career like hers and the odds went even higher against finding that perfect guy at the perfect moment.

It was all well and good to fantasize about a man like Hake El Aran. But one thing she knew for sure: he would never love anyone except himself, and surely not a woman like her.

Hake was losing his mind. Casey had pulled back from him abruptly and completely, and nothing he could say or do seemed to get through to her. Here he was, falling in love with the woman, and she acted as if she wanted nothing to do with him. Women were the most contrary and incomprehensible creatures on the planet!

The next several days settled into a steady and infuriating pattern. They avoided each other during the day. At night, he took her out to the sexiest, most crowded venues he could find. They all but made love to each other in public, and each time magic swept over them, transporting them to a special place where only the two of them existed. It was extraordinary. He fell in love a little more with her each night…and returned to their hotel room at dawn each morning where she retreated to her bedroom alone.

When he confronted her, she made lame excuses about not wanting to ruin her reputation, or she claimed to need to concentrate on the mission. The mission was to *be* his girlfriend, dammit, not just play-act it for a few hours each night! If she did deign to join him for a meal, she treated him with polite disdain as if they were total strangers. It was maddening.

Every trick of seduction he tried backfired more spec-tacularly than the last. He sent her a dozen red roses, and she gave them to the maid. He sent her ten dozen red roses, and she donated them to a local hospital. He sent her an expensive necklace, and he found out from one of the bodyguards that she'd returned it to the jeweler and donated the money to a women's shelter. He considered buying her something truly outrageous like a sports car or a jet, but in his heart he knew that wouldn't be any more effective than what he'd already tried.

Finally, in desperation, he went to Tomas. "Do you happen to have the phone number of the women Casey works with?" he asked his man.

Tomas was alarmed. "Is there a new threat I should know about, sir?"

Only to his sanity. He shook his head. "Nothing like that. It's personal."

Understanding lit the guard's eyes. "Ah. Do you want her boss or her best friend?"

How was it that his men knew who her best friend was and he didn't? He frowned. "The best friend."

"That would be Roxi. Here's her cell phone number."

Hake waited impatiently until it was a semi-civilized time to call someone in the United States, and then he dialed the woman's number.

"Hello?" a cautious voice answered at the other end.

"Hello. This is Hake El Aran."

"Is everything all right? Is Scorpion in trouble?" the woman asked in quick alarm.

"I'm the one in trouble," he replied grimly.

"What's happening?"

"I'm crashing and burning—"

"Say your location," she interrupted tersely. "I'll have emergency response en route immediately."

"No, no. I'm crashing and burning metaphorically."

"Excuse me?"

"I called you to get some advice. About Casey."

"Are we talking romantic advice here?" The woman sounded incredulous. Frankly, so was he that he was making this call.

"Well, yes," he admitted.

There was a long pause. Then a slow chuckle. Then an outright laugh. He endured it grimly, determined to figure out once and for all what had changed Casey's tune for the worse.

Finally the woman's mirth mostly subsided. "Striking out with our girl, are you?"

"In a word, yes."

"And you want my help getting through to her?"

"Yes," he bit out.

"Let me ask you this, Mr. El Aran. What makes you think you're good enough for her?"

His back stiffened. "I beg your pardon?" What was she talking about? Women all over the world were after him. He was a prime catch...wasn't he?

Her voice interrupted his indignant thoughts. "Why should I help you?"

The question startled him. "Because I want her."

"And you always get what you want?"

He didn't answer the question, stung.

"There's your first problem. Casey's not the type to go for arrogant men. She's a strong, independent woman. She wants a partner, not a lord and master."

"I don't boss her around—" he started.

"I'm sure you don't. She'd kick your butt if you tried."

He closed his eyes and took a deep breath. He would suffer through this humiliating conversation if it was the last thing he did. He was at his wit's end. "Tell me more about her."

"She's had exactly two boyfriends in her life that I'm aware of. She was engaged to both. One ultimately couldn't handle her being hired by the FBI. The other couldn't handle her becoming a soldier."

Hake frowned. Her career was so important to her that she'd sacrificed two men she loved for it? He'd had no idea. "What else?"

"Look. This is none of my business, Mr. El Aran. I trust her judgment. If she doesn't like you, she probably has a pretty good reason for it."

"But what reason?" he ground out, as much to himself as to the woman at the other end of the line. "She hasn't told me what it is."

"Have you asked her?" Roxi asked. "The women in our

unit can be a bit more direct than most. Too much of what we do is life-and-death stuff. We can't afford to pussyfoot around issues that come up."

He cringed at the idea of baring his soul to Casey. It went against everything he was. His life had been one long fight for privacy.

When he remained silent, Roxi said gently, "If you won't let her in, why should she let you in?"

Still he said nothing. Roxi made one last comment. "Casey is one of very few women working in an entirely male world. We all have had to fight tooth and nail to gain the respect of the men around us, to deserve and get equal treatment. If she's fought so hard to eliminate a double standard in her career, surely you can't expect her to abide by a double standard in matters of the heart."

He made a noncommittal sound, his mind running far ahead of the conversation at hand.

"Good luck, Mr. El Aran. I hope I've been of some assistance to you." The line went dead in his ear. He stared at the instrument for a long time.

He could accept Casey's career. And to his shock, he could even wrap his mind around making a long-term commitment to her. But she expected him to open his heart to her completely, with no reservations?

No way. He couldn't do it.

Casey was getting tired of the jet-set life. Quickly. The great clothes and fancy clubs were all starting to look the same. No wonder the celebrities in the tabloids always seemed so bored. They were. The late nights didn't agree with her, and waiting for someone to try to kill Hake grated on her nerves. And then there was the man himself. Fighting the jumble inside her of lust and simultaneous urge to kill him made thinking coherently a challenge.

But she knew not to give in to any of it. The more time she spent with him, the more obvious the man didn't have the first clue how to conduct an actual relationship.

She dragged herself out of bed at nearly noon yet again and dressed in a pale yellow dress that reminded her of something she might have worn to Easter church services as a little girl. According to Roxi and her French stylist pal, though, it was appropriate attire for the polo match she and Hake were slated to attend this afternoon. At least Hake had relented on the subject of playing in the match. He'd been determined to ride until his father was finally recruited to call and talk him out of it.

Hake had been surly ever since that call yesterday. Not that she blamed him. It would bug her to death if her father tried to control her life at her age.

She paused in front of her door, going through the daily ritual of girding herself to face Hake. His sheer beauty never failed to hit her like a sucker punch to the gut. She threw open the door and marched into the main room. Oh, Lord. He wore a white linen suit with the palest of pale blue shirts. His tie was pale blue and white striped. From head to toe, he looked like a royal prince. She gulped and hoped desperately that he didn't notice the check in her stride when she'd spotted him.

"Good morning," she murmured distantly.

"Good morning, Casey. How are you feeling today?" he asked mildly.

She started over the distinctly different note in his voice. It alarmed her. She felt much safer when he was all but humming with frustration. "I'm fine, thank you. And you?"

He nodded slowly. "Better."

"Better than what?" she asked cautiously.

"Hungry?" he asked, blatantly ignoring her question.

"I guess so."

"Would you like to dine out on the terrace? It's a lovely day."

What the heck was going on with him? He hadn't been this polite to her in days. "Uh, sure. If Tomas thinks it's safe."

"I already cleared brunch on the terrace with him. He muttered something incomprehensible about sight lines and high ground but declared it safe."

Casey smiled. Since the resort was one of the tallest buildings in the city, the penthouse would, indeed, be difficult to shoot at. Hake held open the door for her, and she slipped by him, concentrating with all her might on not reacting as she passed close to him.

She craved their nights on the town like she craved air to breathe. She counted the hours until she could let go of her precarious self-control and crawl all over him, kissing him and putting her hands on him and giving herself to him the way she wanted to.

Not here, she thought sharply. They weren't out in public. She had to behave until then. *Not yet.*

Check that. *Not ever.*

Hake seated her himself, forcing her to brush past him again. She was intimately familiar with his scent now, but it still sent a rush of excitement up her spine.

"I took the liberty of ordering up brunch for us," he said quietly. "I don't mean to presume, but I thought you might not want to wait for the meal to be prepared. If you don't like what I chose, by all means, feel free to order something else."

She gazed at him quizzically. "What are you up to?"

A faint frown crossed his face, but then his features settled back into patience. "I haven't been exactly good company the past few days, and I owe you an apology."

"You have a lot on your plate," she commented carefully.

"But that gives me no right to treat you badly. You're in as much danger as I am and certainly under as much pressure as I am."

She shrugged. "It's my job. I'm accustomed to functioning under high levels of stress."

"Tell me more about your work."

She frowned. "Why do you ask?"

"It's important to you. Therefore, I'm interested in it."

"What do you want to know?"

"Tell me about these women you work with."

Crud. Not territory she wanted to explore too deeply. "Some women work in the Special Forces. I'm one of them."

"What's that like? Do the men treat you all right?"

She laughed shortly. "What are you going to do? Beat them up if they don't?"

"If you need me to. But I suspect you could teach them a lesson all by yourself without any help from me."

She leaned back in her chair, studying him intently. Why the sudden and complete change in his attitude? Was this some new head game from him? A new and improved tactic to maneuver her back into his bed?

He leaned forward. "Casey, I'm sorry for whatever I've done to make you angry and uncomfortable. I know this business of publicly posing as my girlfriend has been difficult for you, but I wanted to tell you I think you've done a magnificent job."

She glanced down at the stack of gossip rags beside his plate. "How many did we make it into today?"

"All of them. We're the hottest gossip in Europe. They're starting to talk about your career as a dancer."

"Have they called me a stripper yet?" she asked drily.

He threw her a sympathetic glance. "A few have. Sorry."

"Why? It's exactly what we were hoping for. The more sensational your behavior, the more it'll infuriate our terrorists. Dating a stripper, and an American one no less, is quite a slap at the terrorists' extremist values."

"I hope you know I don't think of you that way."

She stared at him, startled. It dawned on her all of a sudden that she did think he saw her that way. Furthermore, it had been sticking in her craw for the past week or more. Was she starting to see herself as some kind of high-priced call girl, throwing herself at him indiscriminately every night?

He grimaced. "I can tell by your expression that you don't believe me. I really am sorry we have to…perform… the way we do in public." He added, "I won't deny that I enjoy our flirting. You, of all people, know exactly how much I enjoy it. I only wish we could be more private about it. It's disrespectful to you."

She shrugged, stunned. "It's the nature of the beast," she mumbled.

"For the record, I do respect you. I think you're smart and classy, and you deserve better than this. If only I could be the man to give it to you."

And with that salvo, he got up and left the table. She stared at his back in shock. What did that mean? Did he still want her for real? Or maybe he'd just told her he was giving up on trying to get her back into his bed. Common sense chose the latter.

Tears stung at the backs of her eyelids. All of the wildly inappropriate gifts and steamy flirting from him in the clubs might have driven her crazy, but at least she'd known that, at some level, he was interested in her. Who was she kidding? She was still the plain, boring person she'd always been.

She picked at her brunch listlessly but suddenly didn't feel much like eating. She retreated to her room and tried to study a map of the polo club, but it was all a blur. Her phone rang and she pounced on it desperate for a distraction.

"Hey, kid. It's me."

Roxi.

"How the heck are ya, Case?"

She'd known Roxi long enough to hear the false cheer in her friend's voice. Sure, the girl was always perky, but this was too much. "Why do you ask?" Casey asked cautiously.

"Just thinking about you. Did you get the dresses I sent over yesterday? I had to get those from Paris. I gotta say, you're getting expensive to dress. But we have to make each outfit more spectacular than the last if we want to keep the press's attention."

Casey frowned. "Something's up with Hake. He's acting weird."

"Weird how?"

"I think he's sick of me. I don't know if he's going to be able to keep up the boyfriend-girlfriend charade much longer. I think you need to warn the gang to start thinking up a Plan B."

Roxi laughed. "Not a chance."

"You should've seen him this morning," Casey said glumly. "He was all distant and polite. He wanted to talk about my job, of all things. It's the kiss of death, I tell you."

Roxi laughed harder. "Good for him."

"Excuse me?"

"The only kind of sick your boy is would be *lovesick*."

"Have you lost your mind?" Casey demanded.

"Chica, he called me yesterday, hat in hand, to ask for advice."

"About what?"

"About you, Einstein."

Casey's jaw fell open. "Oh, my God. What did you tell him?"

"I told him you don't like arrogant jerks, you take your career very seriously and you expect unconditional commitment from the men you commit to."

"No wonder he treated me like I had horns coming out of my head and a third eye in the middle of my forehead just now."

"Girlfriend, you've got him completely off balance. He doesn't know which end is coming or going."

Puh-lease. Hake off balance? Over her? Not in this lifetime. She forced herself into soldier mode and replied seriously, "I don't want him off balance. We need him alert and focused. I think our terrorists will strike soon. They've got to be gnashing their teeth at the shenanigans he and I have been up to."

"Any shenanigans happening off camera?"

Casey snorted. "No. I've been ducking and weaving like a prizefighter to keep it that way, though."

"Maybe you shouldn't dodge so hard. He sounds truly smitten with you."

"You don't know Hake El Aran. He snaps his fingers and women come running. I'm not about to be at his beck and call. The two of us would never work."

Roxi sighed. "Too bad. He seems like the kind of guy who, if he opened up to a woman, would be a heck of a catch."

"That's a big if. An impossible if. He'll never open up to anyone," Casey retorted. She didn't mean for the comment to sound bitter, but she feared it did.

"Well, hang in there, kiddo. And keep your chin up. No telling what'll happen."

Casey scowled. "In our line of work, we're supposed to anticipate events before they happen. And I'm seeing a big fat nothing in my future where Hake El Aran is concerned."

"You know what they say—love is blind."

"Ha. Hake is *so* not in love with me."

"Time will tell."

"Stuff it, Rox."

Laughing, her friend ended the call, leaving her scowling at herself in the mirror. She was *not* in love with Hake. Far from it. She wasn't even in *like* with him.

A quiet knock sounded upon her door. Hake's voice floated through the panel. "Casey, it's almost time to leave. Do you need a few more minutes?"

She checked her hair and makeup quickly. Both were fine. She opened the door to frown at Hake. Since when did he fetch her personally for their dates? He held out his arm to her gallantly.

Lovesick, huh? No way.

Chapter 14

Hake idly watched the polo ponies charging up and down the field. The match was actually a good one with a top Spanish team matched against the ever-powerful Argentineans. However, he couldn't seem to keep his mind on the action. His thoughts kept straying to the woman beside him.

She'd reacted with caution toward him at brunch, suspicious of his change in attitude. He supposed he couldn't blame her. If only he knew what she was thinking right now. But no such luck. The woman was a mystery.

How could Casey think that men were only good for one thing? Outrage at the notion soared through him yet again. He was intelligent. Highly educated. Successful. The kind of man any woman would be proud to have.

Sure, the irony of her observation wasn't lost on him. Casey treated him like he treated most—okay, all—women. But that was how the world worked. Men like him attracted a certain kind of woman, and the formula was always the same. Beautiful, ambitious woman seeks rich, handsome, successful man. She would give him all the sex and domestic backup for his career he needed, and in turn, he would provide a lavish lifestyle for her. There was nothing wrong with that, if everyone got what they wanted. Just because he hadn't entered into such an arrangement so far didn't mean it was a bad business model. He merely hadn't found the right woman yet.

A tiny voice in the back of his head suggested that the vast majority of the women he'd dated over the years would have been thrilled to live out that exact relationship model with him. He shoved the thought away, irritated.

What did Casey want anyway? True love? A soul mate? A man who would worship the ground she walked on? Well, she could look somewhere else, then, thank you very much. Women groveled for him. Not the other way around. *Liar, liar, pants on fire.*

Damn that little voice in the back of his head anyway. He *wasn't* missing any important point here! He liked his life just the way it was. He enjoyed the women in his life just the way they were. Except for the woman in his life right now. He wanted to understand her. To know her. To get what it was she expected of him. *But are you prepared to deliver what she wants?* All right, that little voice could shut up now.

When this cursed deal was done and his family safe once more, Casey would go her own way and he would get back to his life. And by then, his father would have forgotten all about this stupid business of forcing Hake to marry.

"Everything all right, Hake?" Casey murmured, leaning over and placing a hand high on his thigh, ostensibly to balance herself. The touch was intimate and possessive and set his blood on fire.

He forced a smile for her. "I'm fine. Enjoying yourself?"

"I had no idea polo was so rough, with the horses slamming into each other like that. It's like hockey, but on horseback."

He smiled. "That's an excellent analogy."

She leaned closer to him, and his arm naturally went around her shoulders. She snuggled against his side, and damned if she didn't feel exactly right there.

He murmured, "What would you like for dinner?"

She made a sound that could've been a laugh, or maybe half a sob. "Some privacy."

"Done," he answered promptly. Profound relief coursed through him. The idea of having Casey entirely to himself, to treat her the way she deserved to be treated for once, was a breath of fresh air to him. He glanced over his shoulder. "Tomas, Casey and I will be dining in, tonight. Could you ring up the hotel and have them prepare something special for two?"

"Of course, sir."

Hake did his best to ignore the grin on his security chief's face.

Tomas stood up. "I'm not getting cell phone coverage here. I'll be back in a moment."

A tiny frown crossed Casey's brow. She reached into her purse and pulled out her cell phone to check it. Her frown deepened. "Are you getting cell coverage, Hake?"

He fished out his phone and glanced at its face. "No. Why do you ask? We're probably just in a dead spot between towers."

"My phone works off satellites and so does Tomas's—"

And that was when all hell broke loose. An odd whoosh

sounded nearby, followed by four loud explosions so close together they sounded like a string of firecrackers but much, much louder. Glittering flecks of something flew in every direction. That was all Hake saw before Casey's weight threw him over backward in his chair. And then the screaming started. Horses and humans, men, women and children, all screaming. It was a horrible sound.

He didn't need to ask what was going on. He knew. It was the terrorists.

Casey rolled off him and bit out, "Injuries. Report!"

All but one of Tomas's men responded. Hake craned his head and looked up to see blood covering several of his bodyguards. But then Casey was snapping orders again. "Claude, Thierry, you're on Franz. Help him if he's alive. Get him to a hospital and see to your own wounds when you get there. The rest of you, on me and Hake. Let's go."

Franz had been sitting directly in front of Hake. Whatever had sliced the man to ribbons had been aimed at *him*. Cold horror washed over Hake. Just like the night of the restaurant bombing, Casey put a protective hand on top of his head and dragged him along in a half-crouching run. Tomas came up, panting, along his right side.

"Bounding fragmentation mines," the Swiss man grunted.

"I know," Casey replied. "I've run into them before."

Where in the hell had she run into something like that? The disjointed question stuck in Hake's head, probably some sort of mental buffer in lieu of the revulsion and shock trying to crowd their way into his mind.

"The limo?" Tomas bit out.

"No!" Casey answered sharply. "Hake's the target. It could blow. Into the city."

"On foot?" Tomas squawked.

"Will they expect that and be prepared for it?" Casey retorted.

"Good point. But we're down on men."

Hake thought he glimpsed a humorless grin flitting across Casey's face. "But not on women. As soon as we get beyond the terrorists' cell phone jamming, we'll have plenty of backup."

They ran in silence then. *Ran* being the operative word. He was huffing hard to keep up with the blistering pace Casey set. They sprinted the length of the huge polo field, past the barns and parking lot, and burst out onto a city street. Sirens began to wail. It was eerily reminiscent of that first attack in London.

"C'mon," Casey ordered. She moved in front of him, taking point as one of the other men slid in beside him. She continued to run at a breakneck pace, turning corners and crossing streets unexpectedly, making cars slam on their brakes and honk their horns. But always, she pressed forward, deeper into the heart of Nice. After maybe ten minutes, she gave a grunt of satisfaction and ducked into a bookstore. She raced toward the back of the place, startling several customers. She barged through a door marked Employees Only, and blessedly stopped.

Hake caught his breath while she rapidly dialed her cell phone. "Scorpion, here. The attack happened. The principal is unharmed and with me. We've got one man down, possibly dead. I left two men behind to render aid. I have five men with me and the principal. I need a safe house and quickest route from my current position. Request immediate backup from the Medusas."

Medusa? Hake frowned. The original man-hating woman with snakes for hair?

"Roger. Copy." And then Casey tucked her phone back

into her pocket. She shoved a wireless earphone into her left ear and gestured for them to move toward the rear exit.

"Where are we going?" Hake asked.

"Someplace safe. We'll hook up with my team there."

"These Medusas?" he asked curiously.

She gave him a sour look. "Yeah."

They ran for a few more minutes but didn't attract much attention in the growing chaos. Word of the attack was spreading fast across town, and the traffic had come to a standstill as emergency vehicles and bystanders made their way to the scene of the explosion.

Casey careened around a corner and ducked into a doorway without warning. She hustled him and the others inside and slammed the door shut. She spent several long minutes peering out the door's peephole. Finally, she announced, "We're clear."

Tomas and Hake traded relieved looks and the Swiss man muttered, "Damn, she's good. Where did you find her?"

"She found me," Hake grunted back.

"Hell, if you don't marry her, I will," Tomas commented under his breath. Hake wasn't sure he was supposed to have heard the comment and he chose not to respond. But his gut twisted hard at the notion of another man having Casey.

She took off again, racing up the stairs, gesturing them to follow. The woman's stamina amazed him. He kept up with her on pure adrenaline at this point. The attack hadn't gone at all as planned. The terrorists were supposed to show themselves when they tried to kill him, not leave anonymous land mines buried in a polo field to shred everyone indiscriminately.

Casey knocked on an apartment door on the fourth floor and it opened immediately. He and the others raced inside. He came to a halt in the middle of a living room that looked like a military surplus store. Weapons and electronic gadgets were neatly stacked all around the room. Several phones sat on the dining-room table, holding down the corners of a detailed map of Nice.

"Welcome to the snake den," a tall, blonde woman said drily.

"I know you!" Hake exclaimed. "You were in London. Told my men how to do their jobs!"

She held out her hand. "I'm Monica. Nice to meet you. Sorry it has to be under these circumstances."

Hake recognized the almost imperceptibly quick up and down she gave him, noting his brand of watch, the designer who did his suit. This woman was someone intimately familiar with his world. She knew the rules of engagement with men like him. But then the look was gone, replaced by grim focus.

"Early reports are that four bounding fragmentation mines were buried at the edge of the polo field," Monica said tersely. "At least ten dead. A hundred or more wounded. You guys were lucky to get out of there with only one man down."

"Any word on Franz?" Tomas asked quickly.

An Asian woman, who had a phone plastered to each ear across the room, answered, "He's at a hospital. Alive on arrival. Multiple severe lacerations and serious blood loss."

"Speaking of which—" the Asian woman stood up "—any injuries among you in need of a medic?"

"Who are you?" Hake asked.

"Cho. Medic."

Short on words, too, apparently. And then Casey's hands were on him, running over his limbs, across his belly, down his back. "Anything hurting?" she murmured.

He shook his head. "I'm fine. Yet again, your lightning-fast reflexes saved me."

"Franz took the brunt of the shrapnel meant for you. He's the one who should get the credit."

"I pray he lives so I can thank him," Hake replied quietly. Their gazes met in tense understanding. "Are you injured?"

She stopped for a moment, thinking. "No. I was behind Franz, too."

Several of the other men, however, had superficial wounds in need of care, and Cho set about cleaning and bandaging them.

Monica spoke up briskly, "What's the plan now?"

Casey sighed. "Well, that didn't work out the way we wanted. The terrorists outsmarted us and didn't show themselves. Only way we're going to get close to them, apparently, is to go through with the sale of the milling machine."

Monica shrugged. "At least we've got their psychology nailed. We thought we could provoke them to attack and we did. That's good, at any rate."

"Small consolation," Casey muttered. "Viper briefed yet?"

A compact brunette with a single, shocking red streak of hair over her right ear replied, "H.O.T. Watch is on the horn with her right now in Bhoukar. No attacks on the El Aran compound. So it wasn't a coordinated hit. This was definitely retaliation for Hake's antics."

"Which one are you?" Hake asked the punk rocker chick.

"Roxi," she replied. "Or you can call me Hornet."

Ah. The giver of excellent romantic advice. He made eye contact with her and nodded. She grinned back and then turned away quickly.

A beautiful, Persian-looking woman strolled out of another room. "Satellite imagery is chaotic. It'll take hours to I.D. everyone in the vicinity of the polo field. My guess is the mines were placed last night, or even earlier, and went off on timers. H.O.T. Watch is working on recovering telemetry from the past day or two that covers the polo grounds."

Casey made the introductions. "Hake, this is Naraya."

"What's her bug name?" he asked wryly.

Casey smiled. "Black Widow."

Hake nodded. "Any other dangerous insects I should know about?"

"Cho goes by Dragonfly and Monica's handle is Mantis. Tarantula is around somewhere. Her name's Alex, if you prefer."

Monica-Mantis murmured without looking up from the map of Nice, "Her turn to sleep."

Hake frowned. How could a person sleep through all this chaos? Although truth be told, the apartment was pretty quiet. He was the one in the chaotic state.

"Anyone thirsty?" Cho asked.

The women all grinned. He looked at Casey askance and she explained, "One of the symptoms of shock is pathological thirst."

Now that he thought about it, his mouth was as dry as cotton. He indicated he'd like a drink and added, "It's also a symptom of some woman running a guy all over town."

Casey smiled, holding out a two-liter water bottle to him. "That, too." He took it and cracked it open, promptly downing it in its entirety. Tomas and the other men had congregated around the table where Monica was briefing them. They looked rapt. Whether they were impressed with what she was saying or more impressed by the stunning woman delivering it, he couldn't tell.

"Would you like to rest, Hake?" Casey murmured. "There's a bedroom free at the moment."

"Show me where it is?" he murmured back.

Her gaze snapped up to his, but she merely commented, "This way."

He followed her down a long hallway which appeared to have no less than four bedrooms opening off it and a surprisingly large bathroom by French standards. She turned into the last room on the left and held the door for him. He passed by her and she pulled the door shut behind them both.

"You okay?" she asked.

"I'm rattled. It's not every day someone wants me dead bad enough to blow up a whole field full of people and animals to get me."

She sat down on the edge of the bed and picked up the TV remote on the nightstand. She turned on the television and he sat down beside her, numb, to watch the breaking news coverage. No mention was made of him, and that was just fine with him. The images of the polo field were bloody and hard to look at.

"How did we escape with so little harm?" he asked in disbelief.

She shrugged. "You weren't sitting on a horse unprotected, and you let Franz have the front-row seat you normally would have taken."

"I sat in the second row so I could be close to you," he commented, feeling a little detached from his body.

"I'm glad you did," she replied fervently.

"Any idea what's going to happen next with us?" he asked.

She looked up at him sharply, as if questioning how he meant that question. Frankly, he wasn't quite sure how he'd meant it. She chose to answer in a professional context rather than a personal one. "I expect we'll abandon the business of trying to draw an attack to you."

His stomach dropped like lead. "You're not going to leave me, are you?"

She blinked, startled. "I don't know what will happen next. My guess is a team will take you home to Bhoukar to join your family. It consolidates the security coverage, and I doubt the terrorists want to take out both you and your father simultaneously. They need someone alive with whom to do the deal."

"I haven't been to Bhoukar in years. I do not consider it my home," he replied woodenly.

"Nonetheless, I'm betting that's where you'll be headed next."

"When will we know?"

"There will be some sort of teleconference before long. Then as soon as transportation can be arranged, we'll move you."

"Are we looking at a day or two?" he asked grimly.

"More like an hour or two. If that much."

"What will you ladies do with all that gear in the living room?"

"We'll take it with us to wherever we end up going next, of course. We can have that stuff packed in a van in a few minutes."

He snorted. "I've never met a woman yet who can pack for anything in under an hour."

That made her grin. "We can pack to deploy for ninety days in ten minutes."

"Are you sure you're really a woman?" he demanded.

The humor left her face as abruptly as if he'd slapped it off her. He stared, startled. "Surely you know I was joking."

"Of course." Her lips moved and sound came out, but there wasn't even a hint of conviction in her words.

He wrapped his arms around her, drawing her close to him. She was so familiar to him, and yet it felt entirely strange to hold her like this in the privacy of a bedroom. This was real. He kissed her gently. At least at first. As always when they kissed each other, the room quickly disappeared and nothing was left but the two of them straining toward one another, lost in their own world of passion and blinding need.

He murmured against her lips, "I've never met another woman remotely like you. You're a warrior by day and all woman by night. You're smart and capable and take charge in a crisis, but you cuddle against me like a kitten and make me feel like the king of the world when you do. You're as at ease with a gun in your hand as a mascara brush."

"Makeup brushes terrify me," she mumbled against his neck.

He smiled back. "You laugh in situations that most women would fall apart in."

"Yeah, but I fall apart in situations most women would sail through, so it all evens out."

He drew back enough to gaze down at her. "Like when?"

"Like every time we came back to your hotel room after kissing and groping each other all evening. I didn't have the slightest clue how to tell you how much I wished it could continue behind closed doors."

"You wanted to be with me?" he demanded. "Why on earth didn't you say so? I thought you hated my guts after I needed to be alone that first night in Nice."

"What was that all about anyway?" she demanded back.

"Things were moving so fast with us. I was messed up in the head. Had to sort a few things out."

"Like what?"

"Like whether or not I was developing real feelings for you."

She said nothing. Most women would jump all over a comment like that and want to know what he'd decided. But she was not most women. "Don't you want to know what I figured out?" he asked.

"Do you want to tell me?"

"I have real feelings for you," he announced.

"Oh."

He frowned. "Is that all you've got to say to my big declaration?"

"A big declaration of what? So you have feelings for me. They could be feelings of dislike and distaste."

"Difficult woman," he grumbled. He exhaled hard. "I think I'm falling in love with you, for crying out loud."

"Oh." A pause. "Oh!"

He felt slightly better. She at least had the good grace to appear shocked.

"Are you sure?" she asked.

"I'm not sure about anything. I've never done this before. I don't have any idea what falling in love feels like. But I can't sleep at night for wanting to be with you. I can't wait to see your face when I get up in the morning. I want to know what you're doing and thinking and feeling all the time. I feel…empty…whenever we're apart, and I only feel like myself when we're together. You tell me. Is that love?"

She contemplated him thoughtfully. "I don't know. Could just be a bad case of infatuation."

Frustration soared in his gut. "Why are you fighting this?" he demanded. "Aren't you supposed to be happy when someone tells you they love you? And then you declare your feelings back?"

Her detached facade cracked. She said in a small voice, "Mostly, I'm scared to death. This has so much potential to go wrong. And I don't want to get hurt again."

He replied, "Don't all the poets and playwrights say you have to be courageous to risk love? You're the most courageous woman I've ever met, so what's the holdup?"

"I'm a fraud. I'm as scared as the next person. I just know how to mask it better than most."

"You're no fraud. And I'm as scared as you," he said.

She smiled sadly. "We're some pair, aren't we? Most people would be thrilled to discover they're falling in love and rush headlong into it. And here we are, hesitating like complete cowards."

"I'll jump if you will," he said quietly.

She stared at him a long time. And he held his breath for endless seconds. Finally, she said slowly, "Maybe after the mission. When I'm not working with you. When your family's out of danger..."

"You're procrastinating," he accused. "Avoiding the real issue."

Her gaze slid away from his.

"For the record, I'm planning to fight for you," he announced. "And we've already established that I don't fight fair."

That made her look at him warily. "What do you have in mind?"

"A warrior never reveals his tactics to the enemy," he replied grimly.

"Please don't mess with my career," she blurted. "I've worked too hard to get to where I am. Sacrificed too much—"

"Like love? Personal happiness?" he challenged.

Her gaze met his reluctantly. "Yes. Exactly."

"Why can't you have both a career and happiness?"

"That would take a man who fully understands and accepts my work. Who is willing to share me with my career until it has run its course. And with all due respect, Hake, you were raised in a culture where women's needs don't take center stage. I have a hard time believing you're going to be okay with my work at the end of the day."

That gave him serious pause. Finally he said, "You forget I was raised with twelve sisters and a European mother. I was raised to remember to think about the woman."

"Right. And that's why you've been hopping in and out of bed with them by the hundreds. Because you're so committed to their emotional well-being."

"That's not fair!"

"Are you sure it's not?" she challenged.

He paused to consider the accusation. He fought to set aside his defensive reaction. "I was always honest with them. I told them up front that I don't do long-term relationships and not to expect anything more out of me than the moment."

"And yet you wonder why I hesitate to dive into a relationship with you," she retorted drily.

"Things are different between us," he responded with a hint of desperation.

"Because we've nearly died together a time or two? That's just another day at the office in my world, Hake. It's not the basis for lasting love."

"Then what is?" he demanded.

She sighed. "I don't know. I don't have the answers."

He felt everything he'd ever wanted and not known he'd wanted until he met her slipping away from him. "Promise me you'll look for the answers with me. Let's figure this thing out together. Don't close me out until you've given us a chance."

"I don't know—"

"Just don't say no. Withhold a final answer until this thing with the terrorists is over." God, he hated negotiating for his life like this. He was sorely tempted to sweep her into his arms and kiss away her doubts, but he sensed that winning over her mind was every bit as crucial as winning over her body in this fight.

She frowned at him.

"Please. It's not too much to ask." It felt supremely strange to beg. It was not a thing he'd done often—or ever, really, truth be told—in his life.

She sighed. "All right. Fine. I won't decide anything until the mission is wrapped up."

He knew her well enough to believe that she would keep her word at all costs. She was honorable that way. Hence his next request. "Promise me?"

She commented reflectively, "You're getting to know me well if you know to ask that question." She studied him for an endless moment. Sighed. And then said, "Fine. I promise I won't make any decisions about us until the mission's over."

Chapter 15

Casey swore at herself under her breath. Every time her shoulder rubbed against Hake's, her breath caught in the back of her throat. She had to stop reacting to him like this! They were firmly back in her world, on a military transport plane headed for Bhoukar and a showdown with a group of deadly terrorists.

The rules of engagement were entirely different now. She wasn't playing the floozy girlfriend anymore. She was back to being the professional soldier, currently acting as a bodyguard for an extremely important asset. This was a no-fail mission, which meant she and her teammates were under orders to do whatever...*whatever*...it took not to fail. Up to and including killing. Or dying. This was no time to be making goo-goo eyes at Hake.

Although how she was supposed to turn off her feelings and pretend there was nothing between them was beyond her. He was in love with her? *Her?* The thought boggled her mind and did funny things to her stomach every time it occurred to her. She was pretty well head over heels for him herself. She hadn't the slightest idea what to do about it, however.

Ever since the terse teleconference in the apartment where Vanessa ordered them to bring Hake and the milling machine to Bhoukar, a tornado of activity had kept her from thinking about Hake's declaration to her. But now a ten-hour plane ride stretched before her. Hake sat strapped in a web seat in the cargo compartment on her left, and her Medusa team stretched away to her right. The big machine that was the cause of this whole mess sat in a wooden cargo crate at the rear of the aircraft. She shifted in the uncomfortable seat, and her shoulder brushed against Hake's yet again. Her breath caught, and she rolled her eyes in disgust at herself. She was hopeless.

Thankfully, Hake stretched out his muscular legs, crossed him arms over his chest, and closed his eyes. It was easier to think without his steady, warm gaze on her every move.

Roxi leaned close to her. "Chica, roll up your tongue and tuck it back in your mouth, eh?"

She turned to her teammate sharply. "What are you talking about?"

"You can't look at the man without lighting up like a tracer flare. Your whole face glows."

"Crap." She looked glumly at her friend. "What am I supposed to do?"

"Get the job done, and then drag that man to bed and don't get up for a week."

"I don't think a week would be enough between us."

Roxi laughed. "You may be right. He looks at you like he's planning to eat you alive. I knew he was hot for you, but I had no idea."

Casey sighed. "Thing is, you and I both know I can't just dive into the sack with him. Vanessa would have my head on a platter."

"If you two were to become involved seriously, you know, in a real relationship, the boss lady couldn't say much about it. You are allowed to have a personal life after all."

Casey rolled her eyes. "Hake El Aran serious about one woman? How likely is that?"

"I don't know. He looks pretty darned serious about you."

"That's just because I'm so different than a normal woman. I'm still a new and exotic flavor to him."

"Only way to know if that's all it is may be to let him have a good, long taste of you," Roxi said sagely.

Casey glared at her teammate. "Are you advising me to have a torrid affair with him to see if what we have is real?"

Roxi watched at her for a long time. Then she said, "What say you, ladies?"

Casey looked down accusingly at the microphone velcroed around Roxi's throat. "Were we on hot mike with the rest of the team this whole time?" she demanded, appalled.

"That would be an affirmative."

Casey groaned. Crap, crap, crap. Her entire team knew exactly how she felt about Hake now? She glared at Roxi. "You had no right—"

"I had every right. It impacts the mission, hence they needed to know." Roxi glared back until Casey's gaze faltered and fell away.

Casey touched her throat mike and transmitted, "All right. Fine. What do the rest of you nosy, pushy pests think about my private life?"

To their credit, her teammates didn't razz her. They seemed to understand the depth of her mortification and dilemma. Interestingly enough, it was Monica—the hard-core man-hater on the team—who finally answered quietly, "Casey, if you think there's a chance you and Hake could have something long-term, it's worth exploring. Don't walk away from the real thing if you two have it. Just wait until after this mission is over to find out, eh?"

Casey glanced down the row of her teammates and they all nodded in agreement. She sighed. "Easier said than done. Hake's prone to setting his own agenda. I may not control the timing of this thing between us. I'll do what I can."

Roxi spoke up soberly. "Promise me that if it's going to get in the way of the job you'll tell us what's going on between you two."

Casey closed her eyes in dismay. It was a reasonable request. But Lord, the humiliation of laying her love life out before her teammates like this. "Okay. Fine. I'll let you all know."

Roxi punched her lightly on the shoulder. "Chin up, kid. At least we're not demanding video."

Casey's gaze narrowed. "I'll kill anyone who tries to film us. I mean it."

The other women threw up their hands as one, laughing.

She caught up on her sleep and got thoroughly sick of the drone of jet engines before her ears finally started to pop, signaling their descent into Bhoukar. Compliments of the emir, they were exempted from clearing customs and hustled Hake straight off the jet and onto a U.S. Navy cargo helicopter, lent to them for the day by an aircraft carrier group in the Gulf of Oman.

Hake spent the short ride to his family's compound

staring pensively out a small, round window at the desert below. She'd never been to Bhoukar, but she'd seen plenty of mission footage from other Medusa forays into the tiny country. She knew exactly what the miles of endless sand below looked like.

The helicopter slowed to a hover and gradually lowered its bulk to the ground. The whop-whopping of the rotor blades began to wind down. Hake started to stand up, but Casey put a restraining hand on his thigh. His muscles went rock-hard beneath her hand and she looked up at him involuntarily. His gaze burned her alive as it met hers.

"We have to get an all-clear before we offload you," she murmured. "Medusa Team One is completing a security sweep of the perimeter as we speak."

"My sisters are going to love having all these girl commandos protecting Father and me. I'm never going to live it down."

She smiled. "It's better than being dead and not having to live it down at all."

"I'm just glad you're with me," he murmured.

Her gaze went to her teammates, but they were all occupied at the exit, checking for threats to their charge. She said back to him, "You and I need to talk. Alone. As soon as it can be arranged without raising any eyebrows."

"I'll see what I can do," he replied, sounding a little surprised.

And then Vanessa Blake's voice came over her earpiece, declaring the area secure and Hake clear to exit the aircraft. Tomas and his men went first, with the Medusas close behind. And then it was her turn to jump out of the helicopter's belly and to the ground, Hake beside her.

She was in Bhoukar.

With Hake. To meet his family. Her stomach clenched in apprehension. She reminded herself sternly that she was also here to keep Hake alive and catch a gang of violent terrorists. Priority number one.

Hake inhaled the familiar, acrid smell of the desert as a blast of hot, dry air slammed into him. He was definitely back in Bhoukar. Like it or not.

Casey touched his elbow and pointed at the massive building looming ahead. He nodded as they all took off jogging toward it. Tomas and his men flanked the front doors as Casey and the Medusas moved inside. Another half-dozen women in full combat gear joined them and the whole party piled into the foyer of his father's palace. They all took up only a small corner of the towering edifice.

Mosaic tiles of lapis lazuli and gold formed an intricate pattern overhead, and twin marble staircases curved upward in front of him. He'd always thought they looked like a woman's arms welcoming her lover.

"Wow," Casey breathed beside him.

He looked at her quickly. He didn't want her to be impressed. It was just a building. And he was just a man. Please, let her not be so dazzled by his family's wealth that she completely lost sight of him. He'd seen it happen more times than he could count. A servant he didn't recognize led them into the home, veering left into the public wing of the palace. To the right were his family's private quarters. It had been so long since he'd been here, he didn't know if he still had his own suite or not. He just wanted someplace he could be alone with Casey to…to what? Seduce her?

No. To court her.

Somewhere on the long flight, he'd come to terms with that shocking notion. He had no idea if things would work out between them or not. But he wanted to find out one way or the other and not let her walk away before they had a chance to explore this thing between them.

Vanessa Blake spoke ahead of them. "Mr. El Aran has been kind enough to allocate us space for our operations and quarters. It's next to his security center. We have plenty of room for you and your men, Tomas. Along with the El Aran family's permanent security personnel, we've established a hard perimeter and are keeping our presence minimal within the palace. Mr. El Aran has requested that we try not to make his home feel like a police state."

Vanessa veered down a hallway and the others followed her. Hake hung back, though, touching Casey on the elbow. She glanced over at him. "Come with me?" he murmured.

She looked up at her teammates. Roxi glanced back at her and nodded. Casey turned to Hake. "Lead on."

They peeled away from the others and soon were alone in the marble mausoleum his family called home. She commented lightly, "If this were my house, I'd have more furniture. Rugs. Maybe curtains on the windows. Some pictures. Something to make it feel a little more..."

"Homey?" he suggested.

She traded understanding glances with him.

He sighed. "It serves its purpose. It's a calculated display of wealth and power, establishing my father's position in society."

"You didn't need all of this to establish yourself as an important man in London. The financial markets took a measurable hit when people thought you were dead."

He smiled. "Oh, I'm not as important as all that. The markets were just worried about a shake-up in El Aran Industries. It is, without putting too fine a point on it, a big company."

"Not to be rude or anything, but where's your family? If the prodigal son came home at my house, there'd practically be a parade to meet him."

Hake glanced over at her, interested. "There's a prodigal son in your family? Does that mean you have a brother?"

She scowled back at him. "That's not the point."

Someday this woman was going to tell him everything about herself. Until then, he just had to be patient. He shrugged. "I may work with my father, but we are not... close. And the women in the family will not insult him by flocking to greet me before he does. He will greet me formally later."

"And you think having some belly dancer for a companion isn't going to insult the living heck out of him?" she replied gently.

Hake's gaze narrowed. "I am my own man. It's high time my father learned that."

She sighed. "Been there. Done that. Got that T-shirt. Thing is, he's your father. He loves you. He wants the best for you. Don't be so fast to shove me in his face."

Hake stared down at her, surprised. She was the last person he'd have expected to take his father's side. "If you're so determined to be his champion, what do you suggest I do?"

"Greet your father alone. Let me be introduced with the rest of my team as just another one of your guards. There's plenty of time later to make him aware of whatever else there may be between us."

Hake's jaw tightened. He despised her talking about their feelings for one another as if they were hypothetical. This thing between them was real, dammit. He'd done superficial and meaningless so many times he knew the difference.

"Where are we going?" she asked curiously.

"To see if I still have a room in this monstrosity for that private talk you requested. Plus, you can freshen up a little before you meet my family."

"In other words, I stink, huh?"

He laughed. "I suspect we both smell like jet fuel. And no, you don't stink, my dear. You're as lovely as always."

She smiled warmly at him. "That's one of the things I like best about you. You're always such a gentleman."

"I try. Although I'm not sure I always succeed."

She looped a hand in the crook of his arm. His gut tightened like it always did when she touched him. "Trust me. You succeed." And then she started as if just realizing she'd taken his arm and jerked her hand away.

He captured her fingers and put them back on his arm. "I like your hand there."

"I guess it became a habit when we were going out all the time. I don't want to offend anyone in your country, though."

"No one will be offended. Relax. It's just like being in London."

She appeared doubtful as they rode an elevator up to the third floor in silence. He led her down another impossibly long hall to a pair of gilded double doors. He threw them open, not sure what to expect.

His room was exactly as it had been the day he left a decade ago. The bed was made and fresh flowers stood in vases around the room, but it was still his space, complete with his books and maps and treasures collected from his boyhood travels.

"This room looks like you," Casey murmured.

"And how would that be?"

"Masculine. Elegant. Sophisticated."

"A bunch of books and trinkets are all that?" he commented in surprise.

She smiled. "Yes."

"May I offer you a long, hot soak in my Jacuzzi? There isn't one downstairs."

"You do know how to tempt a woman."

He grinned. "Go. Take your bath. I need to check in with my bankers, and their offices should be open in London by now."

She nodded and disappeared into his bathroom. It felt shockingly right for her to be here with him in this place. She was part of his life. Now, how to convince the lady of that? Time was running out on him.

Casey stepped out of the opulent marble tub, her heart heavy. She knew Hake was wealthy. But this was beyond her wildest imaginings. She would never fit into this world. She could handle Hake's yacht. And when she'd seen pictures in a magazine of his flat in London, which was spacious and chic, she hadn't freaked out. Heck, she'd ridden in the man's Rolls-Royce. But none of it had prepared her for this.

Reluctantly, she pulled on her desert beige BDUs and zipped up her combat boots. She strapped on her utility belt, and today it felt as if it weighed a hundred pounds, the pistol holstered at her right hip a block of lead.

With a sigh, she opened the door and stepped out into the main bedroom. Hake glanced up at her from the huge mahogany desk with a phone to his ear and did a quick double take, eyeing her uniform. But then he did the darnedest thing. He smiled at her. Just a smile. As if it was no big deal to him to see her decked out like a commando.

Shock flowed through her, followed closely by a wave a gratitude for his acceptance. Was it possible that he really might be okay with her career after all? He gestured for her to come sit with him, and she relaxed against his warmth as he took care of a few desultory financial transactions with his lawyer. It was a peaceful, domestic moment between them and she relished it far too much. No doubt about it. Letting go of this man would hurt. A lot.

He wound up the call and she rose to go, but he stood as well, taking her hands in his. He held them away from her sides as he looked her up and down again. "So, the soldier wins out over the woman today, does she?"

She shrugged. "Sorry. I'm on the job. It would look strange if I didn't dress like my teammates."

"You're still magnificent, darling," he murmured.

She smiled, but the expression felt brittle on her face. "This is who I am, Hake. Not that other person you think you know."

He frowned. "Why can't you be both?"

It was a hell of a good question. Why not, indeed? "You do have a way of cutting directly to the heart of a matter," she muttered.

"It's why I'm successful in business," he replied blandly. He leaned down and kissed her lightly on the cheek. "You're not fooling me. I still see the woman hiding beneath the trappings of a soldier. She's not gone under all that gear." He flipped one of her ammo pouches lightly.

She stared as he turned away and continued speaking as if he hadn't just stunned her speechless. "Your cell phone rang while you were in the bath, love. I took the liberty of answering it for you. Roxi asked me to have you call her back when you got out."

Uh-oh. Busted messing around with Hake and she hadn't been in Bhoukar an hour. Except she hadn't done anything with him...yet.

He was speaking again. "I'm going to jump into the shower myself while you make your call."

He disappeared into the dressing room and she dialed her phone reluctantly. "Hey, Roxi. What's up?"

"You two christened his room yet?"

Casey sighed. "There's been no hanky-panky between us, I swear."

"Why the heck not? The guy's smoking hot and so in lust with you he can hardly see straight."

"We've already been over this. I have to leave him alone until after the mission's over."

"Have you told him that?" Roxi demanded.

"Well, no. I was going to, though. It's why I agreed to come up to his room with him."

"We do have a little downtime at the moment. Can't do anything until the terrorists contact us. Maybe you should think of this visit to the palace as a break in the mission. Like halftime of a football game."

If only. Casey sighed. "Mama Viper already gave me the big lecture not to fool around on the job on this mission."

Roxi snorted. "Since when does any Medusa, including our ever-so-stern boss, follow the rules? How do you think she ended up married to her boss anyway? If you want the guy, go get him!"

"You're a bad influence, Roxi deLuco."

"Thank you. I try."

Casey rolled her eyes. "So was there a reason you called, or were you just trying to harass me and interfere with my love life?"

"Vanessa wanted to know where you were. She's scheduled a mission briefing in about five minutes. And she wants you here."

Casey sighed. So much for private time with Hake. "I'm on my way."

The water cut off as she called through the bathroom door, "I have to go to a briefing. I'll see you in a while."

The door opened and he stood there, his bronze skin dripping wet, with only a snow-white towel wrapped around his hips. Ho. Lee. Cow. Move over male cover models.

"I'm sorry. I didn't catch all of that," he said. His words were vague, coming to her as if from a long distance, such was the impact of his appearance on her befuddled brain.

"Uh. Briefing. Have to go."

"Me?" he asked. "They need me at a briefing?"

"Uh, no. Me," she mumbled.

A slow grin started to spread across his face. "Are you all right?"

"No. Not…no."

He reached out of sight beyond the door and came up with a second towel. He strolled forward, commencing to towel his hair. "Never seen a guy get out of a shower before?" he asked casually.

"No…uh…yes…but not…uh…you…"

He stepped close enough to her that she felt the humid heat rolling off his body. "You're cute when you're flustered," he said.

She opened and closed her mouth a few times and finally just shook her head. "This is so not going to work between us."

The towel came off his head. "Why not?" he demanded.

"You and I are from totally different worlds. This all—" she waved her hand to encompass his room "—it's too much. I don't belong in a palace. Everything about you is too—" she searched for a word and finally finished "—perfect."

Warm fingertips traced her jawline lightly and she inhaled sharply.

He said slowly, "Let me get this straight. You want to dump me because I'm too rich?"

"Well, sort of. I mean I don't want to dump you. But I don't see how I could ever learn to live with all of this."

A smile spread across his face and grew brighter and brighter until it nearly blinded her. Or maybe that was just lust blinding her. He said, "Just think of all the time it will take for the two of us to share our worlds with one another. Years. Decades, even. And every moment of it will be interesting and exciting and new for both of us. Tell me you'll give me and all of this a chance—"

She started to lean in to kiss him, mostly in desperation to stop him from completing the question and putting her horribly on the spot, but her phone vibrated in her pocket and saved the day. "I'm late. Gotta run."

She turned and fled without looking back. She was such a *coward*. She was too scared to admit to him just how hard she'd fallen for him, and way too scared to admit it to her teammates. Heck, she was barely able to admit it to herself. Any sane woman would've leaped all over the offer he'd made to her and done everything in her power to land this guy. But she…she was doing everything in her power to drive the guy away from her. What was *wrong* with her? And what on earth was she going to tell him when he lost patience and came right out and demanded to know her intentions toward him?

Chapter 16

Casey listened in dismay as Vanessa went over the details of her latest conversation with Geoffrey Birch. The terrorists had contacted him and were pushing to complete the sale immediately. Vanessa had advised the attorney to agree to the terrorists' terms. The transfer of funds would happen later today. Their teammates at H.O.T. Watch headquarters had a few hours to track the source of the monies and catch the terrorists that way. However, everyone agreed that the odds of the terrorists slipping up and making a mistake in hiding their money trail were extremely small.

Plan B was to go ahead with the transfer of the milling machine.

Tonight.

Casey's heart about fell out of her chest at that news. She and Hake were out of time. Worse, she wasn't mentally prepared for him to be exposed to danger. But unfortunately, the first condition the terrorists had set for the transfer of the machine was that Hake personally deliver it.

As H.O.T. Watch had anticipated, the terrorists expected to move the machine by sea, and they demanded that Hake drive it in a truck to an exact location they would give him later. The rendezvous point could lie anywhere along the coast of Bhoukar, which meant the Medusas would not have long tonight to scout out the meeting locale and get a team in place to protect Hake. For surely the terrorists expected to kill him once he'd delivered the goods. He'd had the gall to survive both of their earlier attempts to kill him; it would be a point of honor not to let him live out the night.

Once the hostiles had the machine, they would no doubt sail for the pirate-infested waters of the Gulf of Aden and the wild and wooly coast of east Africa where it would be easy for them to slip ashore and disappear with their prize.

"What about sabotaging the milling machine?" Casey asked, desperate to delay the handoff. "Is that done?"

Vanessa nodded. "Marat's engineers say it is. I'd like Naraya to take a look at their work herself and verify it, however."

The engineer on their team nodded briskly.

Vanessa diagrammed a rough plan of deployment. "We'll all ride in the truck with the machine, jump out as close to the meet as we can and work our way in on foot."

Roxi asked, "Is the Bhoukari Army going to insist on being there?"

Vanessa shook her head. "Our president and the Bhoukari emir share an extraordinarily close friendship, and the president has asked him, as a favor, to leave this operation entirely to us. Which is to say, the whole mission's on our shoulders, ladies."

Casey looked around the room. She couldn't think of a dozen other people in the entire world she'd rather have this mission depending upon. Forged in blood, sweat and tears, the Medusas had become a single, finely honed weapon, a seamless killing machine. They were tough, experienced and confident. Everything would go smoothly tonight.

Then why were her hands shaking and her innards threatening open revolt at any second? Hake. That was why. He was going to be out there, exposed to the very people who'd tried twice now to kill him.

"Casey, I want you on Hake."

She jerked at hearing her name and stared at her boss in surprise as Vanessa continued, "The terrorists know you. They think you're a bimbo—no offense intended—"

"None taken," Casey murmured.

"And we can use that to our advantage," Vanessa added. "They won't know why Hake brought you along and they won't like it, but they won't be worried by you. You did an excellent job getting yourself portrayed by the press as a harmless party girl."

Casey grimaced. "Gee. Thanks."

As chuckles passed around the table, Vanessa continued, "You'll need to find some sort of clothing that doesn't make you look like a professional bodyguard."

Casey nodded. "I'm sure someone around here can help me with that. What about Tomas and crew?"

"I don't want civilians in our field of fire, no matter how good they are," Vanessa replied briskly. "I'm assigning them to guard our retreat if things go bad. They'll lay down a volley of covering fire and open up an escape corridor if we need one."

Monica spoke up, "What if the terrorists get the machine onto their vessel and make it out of port?"

"That's actually the idea," Vanessa replied. "As soon as

they cross into international waters, the U.S. Navy will be waiting for them. We already have a submarine, a destroyer and three SEAL teams tasked to take these guys. They're loitering off the coast now and are under orders to sink the ship and make our terrorists disappear permanently. Ideally, they'll take a few prisoners for long-term interrogation, but the priority is to kill the ship. Our job is merely to drive the terrorists into their grasp."

Casey asked the obvious next question, "And if the terrorists stay in Bhoukari waters and don't go international?"

Vanessa grinned. "The emir assures us that it's very difficult for his navy to tell where invisible boundary lines in the water lie and he's quite fuzzy on the subject himself."

Vanessa spent the next half hour going over the operational plan for the handoff in excruciating detail. The whole plan centered around showing Hake to the terrorists as briefly as possible and then getting him the heck out of there before anyone could kill him.

Easy as pie. Then why was Casey's gut twisted into so many knots that she could hardly breathe?

Vanessa wrapped up with, "And while we wait for the call to come in, Mr. and Mrs. El Aran have invited us all to dine with them this evening. They're fine with our BDUs, but no weapons at the dinner table, please."

Casey gulped...and then prayed furiously that Hake took her advice and didn't make a scene about her tonight.

As the Medusas piled out of the briefing room and followed Vanessa to a massive dining room that already held nearly fifty people, apparently all of Hake's extended family, Casey made a point of blending into the middle of the pack of women soldiers.

She spotted Hake the instant the Medusas stepped

into the banquet hall. He was standing beside an older version of himself—that must be his father. And the elegant woman with them must be his mother. Even his parents were perfect and intimidating. But then Mr. El Aran smiled and welcomed them all so pleasantly that Casey's shoulders actually began to unhunch from around her ears. Mrs. El Aran, who spoke English with a light Italian accent, waved for them all to be seated and for the meal to be served. The crowd moved toward a giant table spanning the length of the room.

Mrs. El Aran gestured for Vanessa to sit beside her, and Casey was intensely relieved that her boss got diplomatic babysitting duty tonight.

But then Mr. El Aran's voice rang out clearly before Casey could slip into a nicely anonymous seat at the other end of the long table. "Which one of you is the dancer? The one who's been in all the tabloids with my son."

Oh, Lord. Her teammates flashed her sympathetic glances as Casey reluctantly stepped out of their protective midst. Hake's back was ramrod stiff and his jaw seemed about ready to shatter, he was so furious. This was going to turn ugly very fast and very soon.

She forced her feet to carry her toward Hake and his parents. Vanessa looked like a thundercloud beside them. She silently blessed her boss for taking offense at her reputation being questioned in any way. If only she deserved Vanessa's indignation. But she'd crossed the line with Hake, and no amount of scrambling now was going to change that.

Casey cleared her throat. "I would be the dancer, sir."

"Come closer. I want to speak with you, young lady."

Sighing, she calculated the odds of making it to the exit before one of her teammates tackled her and bodily dragged her to face Papa El Aran. Zilch. Maybe when his father was done with her, Hake would finally catch a clue and realize just how unsuited for his life she was.

In the meantime, she was a Medusa. She groveled for no man. Her heart might be breaking, but that didn't mean she was beaten. She lifted her chin and strode forward to face the music. The one thing she dared not do was look at Hake. She'd fall apart if she so much as glanced over at him.

Vanessa caught her gaze ever so briefly, and Casey thought she saw support and encouragement from her boss. Casey neared Hake and his parents, and she glued her attention on his father. The man was studying her intently, as if he were searching for something. "This is the same beauty I've seen splashed all over the newspapers?" he asked incredulously.

Casey blinked. "I beg your pardon, sir?"

"Remarkable. In this attire, you look just like the other lady soldiers. And you're the one who saved his life in that nightclub in London?"

Casey shrugged. "I shoved him under a table. Whether that saved his life or not, I couldn't say."

Hake interrupted. "Don't be modest, Casey." He turned to his father. "She threw herself on top of me to protect me. And she tackled me again yesterday with no regard for her own safety when the mines exploded at the polo field."

Mrs. El Aran startled Casey by stepping forward then and wrapping Casey, BDUs and all, in a hug. "Thank you so much for saving my son's life. How can we ever thank you?"

"No thanks are necessary," Casey mumbled. "I was just doing my job."

"Nonsense," Marat declared. "We are forever in your debt."

"In that case—" Hake started.

Casey cut him off with a glare. She turned to his mother and registered the woman looking back and forth between her and Hake in dawning amusement. Casey said politely, "In that case, Mr. and Mrs. El Aran, let's enjoy a pleasant dinner and you can tell me all about what a naughty child Hake was. After working with him for the past few weeks, I have no doubt he was a handful."

Mrs. El Aran laughed and commenced regaling Casey with stories of Hake's adventurous youth. Hake, who was seated across the table, rolled his eyes and put up with it, but clearly he was impatient with her. Too bad. Until the two of them had some idea of what was going on between them, the last thing they needed to do was involve his family. She was right, and he could just get over it.

Several times he tried to steer the conversation back to his relationship with Casey, and each time, Casey headed him off, smoothly turning the conversation to some other subject. And each time she did it, Hake's jaw clenched harder. She blandly ignored him as he stewed. If she wasn't mistaken, Mama El Aran's amusement was growing by the minute at Hake getting managed by a woman like this.

The food was delicious and the company pleasant, and no more was said of her and Hake's antics in France. But when the formal meal adjourned and everyone milled around chatting, Hake moved to her side and gripped her elbow tightly. He leaned down to growl in her ear, "My room. Ten minutes."

He strode out then, and she didn't watch him go. Really. She wasn't a silly teenager to engage in a secret rendezvous like this. However, almost ten minutes later, she asked one of Hake's sisters where a restroom was and the woman offered to show it to her. Casey smiled and accepted the guide.

The two women stepped out into the grand hallway and

Hake's sister murmured, "Take this elevator to the third floor and turn right when the door opens. Go all the way to the end, and it's on the left."

Casey stared.

"Go on," the woman murmured, smiling. "It's high time my brother found himself a woman who can stand up to him like you do. I haven't seen my parents so delighted in years. Good luck and go with the family's blessing."

The elevator doors closed and Casey stood there in shock. The family approved of her? The belly-dancing commando? No way. She felt like a high-wire performer who'd just had the net pulled out from underneath her in the middle of her show. She'd been so sure his family wouldn't tolerate her anywhere near Hake. Now what was she supposed to do?

Before she hardly knew what was happening, she was standing in front of Hake's bedroom door. What came next? She had no idea. But she did know one thing: she was a Medusa. And Medusas faced their fears head-on. She took a deep breath and pushed open his door.

As she walked in, Hake turned from where he stood by the bedroom window. She spoke sharply, "Unless that's bullet-resistant glass, you should get away from there. And even then, it's not good policy to expose yourself to a sniper. Sometimes they have gear that will punch through the best bullet-resistant materials."

"How do you soldiers say it…you can stand down now?"

"That's how we say it, but I'm not about to stand down. Your safety is my number one concern."

He strode forward, irritated. "Is that what you were doing at dinner? Protecting me? It was the perfect opportunity to tell my father about us. He was inclined to be generous with you and grant you a favor, and you wouldn't let me say a thing!"

"It was not the right time or place," she declared flatly.

"I am not accustomed to being told what to do," he snapped.

She laughed. "Then it must suck being around me and my teammates. Particularly when your life depends on following our orders."

He glared at her for a moment more, but then his irritation broke. He sighed. "I just don't like hiding my feelings for you like this." He commenced pacing, but well back from the wall of windows.

She leaned a hip on his desk. "I don't see anyone we need to hide from right now. Are there surveillance cameras in here I should know about?"

"Heavens, no. The family's private quarters would never be watched."

"Then relax already," she said softly. "You don't have to hide anything from me."

He stopped and stared at her. "I don't, do I?"

Their gazes met. A realization of just how far they'd come unfolded between them. Nervous, she murmured, "I have to brief you on the mission."

"The mission. It's always the mission with you. When are you going to admit to yourself that you're hiding behind all this soldiering stuff?"

She retorted, "When are you going to realize that a soldier is who I *am?*"

"I *am* a banker, but that doesn't mean I'm not a man, too. It doesn't mean I can't have a personal life."

"My work is different," she declared.

"Only if you let it be. You've chosen to let it consume

your life. To let it consume your identity and your femininity."

She glared at him and he glared back. Finally, she stated flatly, "We don't have time for this right now. I have to tell you about the mission." Ignoring his obvious frustration, she launched into a recitation of the plan as it currently stood.

He crossed his arms, plastered on an impassive look and listened.

"Oh, and one more thing," she added. "If they hit me, you have to let them."

That got a reaction out of him. A snort of contempt.

"I'm serious, Hake. These guys think women are worthless, and you need to appear to believe the same."

"Not happening. Nobody hits my woman and gets away with it."

A thrill shot through her that brought her up short. Okay, she was not supposed to get all fluttery over being protected by some man. But still…it felt good that he was protective of her like that. It took a moment for her to collect herself enough to say calmly, "Regardless, you must let them. My life will depend on it and yours, too. They have to believe I'm not important. That I can be ignored."

That garnered another snort from him. "I keep telling you. You're impossible to ignore. When will you get that through your head?"

Another thrill rippled through her. She couldn't think about that right now! Right now, she was a soldier. Not a woman. Why couldn't he see that?

"I have to go check my weapons and scare up some clothes for myself," she said grimly. "I'll be back to collect you when the terrorists call. In the meantime, you should try to get some rest. It could be a long night."

Roxi looked up sharply at her when she stomped

into their impromptu command center. "You all right, Scorpion?"

Casey scowled. She was emphatically not all right. Hake's insistence on reminding her that she was a sexy, desirable woman was distracting in the extreme. "I'll live," she grumbled.

"H.O.T. Watch sent us satellite imagery of the terrain along the coast. You might want to familiarize yourself with it," Roxi said neutrally.

Right. Terrain. She spent the next two hours going through the motions of final mission preparation, but she wasn't at all sure how much of it actually stuck in her head. Hopefully enough. The good news was that the rest of the Medusas would be with her and Hake. She felt perfectly safe in their care.

The call came in at midnight. Hake was to drive the large flatbed truck bearing the milling machine by a specified route to the coastal highway, departing within the next ten minutes, or the transfer was off.

Casey dialed Hake's cell phone. He picked up on the second ring. "It's me," she said briskly. "Time to rock and roll. We need to leave immediately."

"I'm on my way," he replied tersely.

She winced as she hung up. He sounded none too pleased with her. She supposed she couldn't blame him, but there was nothing she could do about it. She knew the mental, physical and emotional demands of a mission and he didn't. But he was about to learn.

Chapter 17

Hake stared in shock as Casey climbed up into the cab of the semitruck beside him. "What in the hell are you wearing?"

She was swathed in black, voluminous robes, her head covered by a matching black scarf that came down low on her forehead. Missing only was the draped scarf across her face. It was a shock to see her like that.

She replied, "Surely you recognize traditional Bhoukari dress. We left my face uncovered so the terrorists would recognize me. But I need the robes to cover my weapons. Remember, try to find a way to send me back to the truck after they've searched me, so I can fetch my toys."

"This is insane. I won't have you exposed to danger like this," he declared.

"What? And I'm supposed to sit home twiddling my thumbs while you charge headlong into the jaws of death?"

"Better me than you," he replied, supremely frustrated that a bunch of terrorists had forced him and everyone who mattered to him into this mess.

She replied soothingly, "I have years of the best training on earth for doing exactly this."

A metallic voice sounded inside his head, emanating from the tiny transceiver behind his last molars on the right. "Listen to her, Hake. She's right." That was Vanessa Blake if he wasn't mistaken. He swore under his breath. He didn't like this one bit. It was bad enough that he was probably driving straight into a trap. But to be forced to bring along the woman he loved…he swore again.

"Do you know how to drive this thing or do you need a crash course?" Casey asked.

"I spent a summer as a teenager driving delivery trucks for my father. He believed it was important for me to see our business from the ground up."

"Smart man," she commented.

"Everyone on board?" he murmured into his mouthpiece.

"We're ready to roll," came Vanessa's response. "And our ten minutes are almost up."

Hake shoved the lever behind the steering wheel, throwing the big truck into gear. "How will the terrorists know if I've left within their time limit?" he asked to fill the empty space between him and Casey.

"We think they're tracking your cell phone signal. Our telemetry shows nobody within the vicinity of the palace who could be doing eyes-on surveillance of you."

"Now what?" he asked.

"Head down the road they told you to."

He drove in silence. The truck's headlights lit a swath of tarmac before him, but everything else—the desert, the sky, the night blanketing them—was an enormous black void. It made a man feel incredibly small. The tension within the cab was palpable. Whether its source was the mission or the unresolved questions hanging between Casey and him, he didn't know. But either way, it was intensely uncomfortable. Finally, he burst out, "Look, if we're about to die, shouldn't we clear the air between us?"

She looked over at him but the scarf covered most of her expression. "I think we've pretty much said it all, don't you?"

"Not by a long shot," he burst out.

In the dim glow of the dashboard lights, she sent him a pleading look and pointed to her mouth and then her ear. He scowled. At this point, he didn't give a damn if her teammates heard everything the two of them said to each other. He was sick of not knowing where he stood with her.

She sighed. "Hake, if you truly want to be with me for the long-term, you need to see this side of me. Consider tonight an up-close-and-personal tour of my world. Let's just wait and see what you think after it's all over."

He considered for a moment. "Fair enough. But in return, I ask that you give my world a try." He added grimly, "With an open mind."

She stared at him for a long time. Finally, she nodded. All right, then. He could live with that. He sat back and concentrated on driving.

After about a half hour, a flurry of talking erupted inside his skull. Apparently the support team for the Medusas had picked up infrared satellite images of a cluster of people arrayed in what looked like an ambush formation a few miles ahead. Most of the chatter made little sense to him, but Casey went tense.

He eased off the accelerator.

"No!" she exclaimed. "Keep going the same speed. The

terrorists are tracking us. We can't signal them that we've spotted the trap or they'll know we're using sophisticated support."

Great. The terrorists were watching him. Her teammates were listening to him. Uncle Sam was looking down on him from space. It could give a guy a complex. The road began to climb and he downshifted to handle the grade. And then a sharp noise sounded from the seat beside him, making him jump violently. His cell phone was ringing.

"Pick it up," Casey said tightly.

He put the device to his ear. "Hello."

A male voice directed without preamble, "There's a bridge ahead. Drive across it and stop on the far side." The call disconnected before he could say anything.

"Got that?" Casey bit out.

"Roger," Vanessa replied. "We'll get out on this side of the bridge and make our way across the obstacle on foot."

An unidentified male voice—must be one of the H.O.T. Watch people—replied in Hake's head. "Negative, Viper. The bridge spans a gorge at least five-hundred-feet deep. Recommend you use the bridge to cross."

Vanessa spoke rapidly to her team. Apparently, they would decide when they saw the bridge whether to sneak across it topside or climb underneath the thing to cross the gorge. In the meantime, she ordered the Medusas to prepare to exit the truck. He looked at his speedometer in alarm. He was still going nearly thirty miles per hour.

"They're going to jump at this speed?" he asked Casey incredulously.

She replied, "It would help if you slowed down a little. Could you make it look like the truck's laboring up the slope a bit more?"

"Done." He downshifted again and the truck slowed to roughly twenty miles per hour.

"That's good," she commented.

As they neared the top of a rocky ridge, Vanessa ordered the Medusas to jump. He looked out his rearview mirrors, trying to spot them as they left, but he saw nothing. He listened to a quick check-in as all the Medusas reported in and regrouped to follow the truck to the bridge. He downshifted one more time, bringing his speed down to under fifteen miles per hour. It was the most he could do to buy the women behind him time to catch up.

The vehicle topped the ridge and Casey gasped. A massive gorge yawned before them. The bridge ahead looked sturdy enough, but the drop on either side of it was impressive.

Casey radioed, "Plan on going under the bridge. There's no superstructure at all to provide cover."

"Roger," Vanessa replied. The woman sounded a little out of breath. Must be running up the last bit of the slope behind them.

"Here goes nothing," he muttered as he guided the truck out onto the bridge. The tires bumped loudly across the steel joints. And then a funny thing happened. Casey seemed to relax beside him. Cool calm rolled off her.

"You all right?" he asked.

She merely nodded, scanning ahead of them. And then she murmured. "Rocky ridges at ten and two o'clock, range from the bridge, two hundred yards. Ideal cover for snipers. Open, flat clearing just beyond the bridge. Two SUVs parked. Four hostiles in sight."

The truck crossed the final few yards of the bridge. Hake applied the brakes and the vehicle came to a halt. He reached for the door handle.

"Don't get out," Casey breathed. "Force them to make the next move."

He nodded and subsided. All of a sudden, a massive flash lit up the night and an enormous impact of noise and concussion rocked the truck. He ducked instinctively, diving across the cab to protect Casey.

"Report!" she bit out frantically.

And then it hit him. The terrorists had just blown up the bridge. Were the Medusas already climbing under it when it went? Had all of her teammates died? And just as worrisome, had their support just been blown up? Were he and Casey completely alone with the terrorists?

Nobody answered her urgent radio call. Casey whispered again, more forcefully, "Report. Is anyone in the clear?"

Eventually, a voice—blessedly female—replied, "We just missed getting obliterated. Cho spotted the explosives and we backed off the bridge just before it blew. We're alive. But we're on the wrong side of the gorge."

His stomach fell like a brick. The two of them *were* alone and without backup. He looked across the cab at her grimly, and she returned the look, fully aware of their predicament.

Hake's cell phone rang. Thinking fast, he picked it up and said angrily, "What the hell are you people trying to do? Blow up your equipment before I can deliver it to you?"

"Get out of the truck. Hands on top of your head," the voice ordered.

"They want us outside. Hands on our heads," he murmured to Casey.

She replied low and fast, "Hit speed dial number nine, then put the phone in your pocket and don't disconnect it."

"Why?" He turned off the truck's ignition and reached for the door.

"I programmed H.O.T. Watch into your phone. They'll be able to monitor our conversation."

Damn, she was good. He did as she'd said and then opened the door. Across the cab, she did the same. He heard a series of ominous metallic clicks that sounded suspiciously like the noise of weapons being brought to bear and readied to fire.

"Did you have to drag me out here in the middle of nowhere, Hake?" Casey complained loudly. "And what on earth was that— Ohmigod! The bridge is gone!"

A man's voice called out, "Who is that? Kill—"

Hake called back, "I had to bring her along. My mother threw her out of the house. She's a belly dancer. She's of no importance."

Disgusted swearing met that announcement. He thought he heard a man say he recognized the girl. But Hake couldn't see a blessed thing. His night vision had been destroyed by that blindingly bright flash of light. He supposed that meant the bad guys couldn't see much better, though.

"All right, gentlemen," he announced. "Let's finish this thing and get you on your way before the army or someone else spots us."

Two men stepped forward, close enough for Hake to see the anger on their faces. "You were not told to bring anyone with you."

"I wasn't told not to," Hake shot back as a man stepped forward to frisk him. "Besides, your people surely know who she is."

The older man of the two looming before him with shotguns in their hands scowled. "You dare to bring that whore to us? How dare you insult us?"

Casey piped up indignantly as a man rudely ran his

hands all over her body beneath her robes. "I'm a dancer, not a whore."

The older man's hand whipped out and he slapped her across the face hard enough to drop her like a stone to the ground. Hake lurched, a snarl building in the back of his throat. But then something strong gripped his ankle and he jumped in surprise. Casey was squeezing his ankle tightly enough to make him grimace. He took a deep breath and released it slowly.

"Gentlemen," he said smoothly. "We are here to conduct a business transaction. Can we not do this in a civilized manner and then be on our way?"

The older man, clearly the leader of this bunch, stared at him assessingly. "Show me the machine."

"Of course." Hake led him to the back of the truck. Two of the terrorists jumped up on the flatbed, quickly unhooked the tarp covering the machine, and threw it back.

"Careful," Hake barked. "That's a piece of precision equipment. Watch it!"

"Show me how it works," the leader demanded.

Hake nodded and climbed up onto the truck bed. He risked a glance over at Casey as the leader joined him. She was back on her feet. Two more men had moved out of the shadows and were pointing guns at her. She seemed to be making conversation with them. At any rate, she had the men's undivided attention.

Hake turned back to the machine and the now eager man beside him. He gave the fellow a fast tour of how the machine worked. Hake used the most technical language he could muster in hopes that the terrorist wouldn't understand much of it.

"At any rate," Hake finished, "it's all in the instruction

manuals. They're in the truck. Cassandra, fetch the notebooks!"

She moved toward the truck and the terrorists let her. Apparently, they thought it perfectly normal to order the woman to do the manual labor. Their mistake. He'd glimpsed the arsenal she'd tucked under the front seat. She emerged from the truck, carrying a tall stack of binders.

"Where do you want these?" she asked humbly enough of one of the junior terrorists.

The fellow directed her to one of the SUVs and she dutifully trudged through the sand to the vehicle. She leaned into the passenger's seat, disappearing from view for a heartbeat too long. Hake suppressed a grin. She'd done something to the vehicle. She exited to the rear, passing behind the first vehicle and brushing past the other SUV. Knowing her, that had also been time enough to do something to the second vehicle. Hake was impressed. Aloud, he said, "My bankers tell me the money transfer is complete. If you'll tell me where we're going next, I'll drive the truck to our destination and load this thing onto your ship."

"We will take the machine from here," the elder terrorist replied sharply.

Hake shook his head in the negative. "This is a delicate piece of equipment. Load it improperly and you'll render it inoperative."

The terrorist scowled and pulled out a cell phone. He climbed down off the truck and moved away from Hake to make a call. Hake took the opportunity to move back to Casey's side. He murmured to her in English, "I told him they'll need me to load the machine onto their ship or they'll break it. He's calling his boss."

She murmured back, "When it's time, head for those rocks to the north. Their snipers are on the south ridge."

That was all they had time for before the senior terrorist strode toward them. "We will handle the loading. Give me the keys."

"A truck was not part of our deal," Hake replied evenly. "Are you prepared to pay for it or return it when you're done with it?"

The terrorist laughed shortly, without humor. "Sure. Whatever."

Hake didn't like the sound of that. These people were planning to kill him sooner rather than later. Had he not known Casey so well, he wouldn't have noticed the subtle tensing of her shoulders. But as it was, he had to consciously stop himself from bracing, too.

The older man stepped close and held his hand out for the truck keys. The sounds, two of them in quick succession, were no more than a gentle spit. A boy shooting a seed from between his front teeth. The terrorist, no more than arm's length from Hake, got a surprised look on his face. Stunned, Hake stepped forward fast and wrapped his arms around the man, staggering under his weight but preventing him from collapsing to the ground.

"Thank you for letting me and my family aid your holy cause," Hake said loudly enough for the other men to hear.

The other men started forward, but were confused enough by the abrupt embrace and declaration to hesitate. It was enough for Casey. She spun and fired from beneath her robe, six shockingly fast and deadly accurate spits. All three men dropped without firing a single round. Hake let his man slide to the ground.

Casey took off running, dodging behind the first SUV. Hake was on her heels. She paused just long enough to point at the ridge behind them. He nodded and they were off and running again, zigzagging low and fast. Casey pulled ahead of him by a few feet and dived over a boulder, disappearing. He mimicked the move, flying over the boulder, slamming into the ground and rolling until he fetched up hard against something warm.

Something pinged over his head and chips of rock flew past his face.

Casey swore softly. "I'd hoped to make the ridge before they pinned us down."

"Now what?" he murmured.

Her only answer was a grim glance. "Any chance I can get some backup in the next two minutes?" she asked whoever was listening to the other end of their radios.

A male voice came back. "Negative. We've got satellites on you and an unmanned aerial vehicle is en route. ETA fifteen minutes."

"That won't help us," she replied tersely.

Hake glanced behind them. Suddenly, the fifty or so feet of open ground before the first rise of the ridge looked miles wide. He peeked around the end of the boulder, trying to spot whoever was shooting at him. Dust flew up in front of him and he lurched backward. He didn't know much about military operations, but even he knew they would have to shoot their way out of this one.

"Have you got a spare weapon?" he asked quietly.

She glanced over at him. Silently, she passed him a pair of pistols from under her robes. "I've got limited ammo. How are you at crawling on your belly?"

Hake answered wryly, "I've never tried it. But if my life is going to depend on it, I'm pretty darned good at it."

The corner of her mouth curved up. "Put on my robe." She stripped the black garment and passed it to him.

As he pulled it over his head, the point of the exercise dawned on him. She wanted him to look like her. She expected the snipers to concentrate their fire on him, so she was trying to switch identities with him. He pulled the robe back off. "You wear it."

"Don't argue with me," she said warningly. "You agreed to follow my orders."

"I didn't agree to let you die for me," he retorted.

"Yes, you did. This is my job. Don't get in my way."

He ground out, "You're also the woman I love. I'm not letting you do this."

She glared at him. "We don't have time for this." She broke off to peek around her side of the boulder for a moment.

More rock flew and the male voice came back in his head. "Movement. Four hostiles. Range one-hundred-twenty yards. They're coming in cautious, staying under cover. One high-powered sniper rig. The other three are using medium-range, vintage rifles."

"Roger," Casey replied. "Best route of retreat?"

"Heading 0—1—0. But you will cross the hostile field of fire."

Hake frowned. That didn't sound good. Casey gave a quick affirmative, however, and didn't look fazed. He looked at her questioningly.

She answered his unspoken question. "Now we wait. We have to pull them in closer."

"Excuse me?" Hake retorted.

"We need a diversion, and I've got just the one. But I need the shooters to move toward us."

"Fake me being injured," Hake suggested.

She looked at him speculatively. "That's actually a good idea. But we're only doing it if you wear my robe."

He scowled. Sometimes in business, a man had to know how to give in gracefully. But he didn't have to like it. He yanked on the robe. "Fine. Now what?"

"I put my arm over your shoulder and we stand up just

enough to be seen trying to limp toward the ridge. Give it, say, three steps, and then hit the dirt. Got it?"

"Got it." She put her arm over his shoulder and he hoisted her to her feet. They hop-skipped a few steps while she pretended to drag a leg behind her, and then they dived together for the ground. Just in time, too, for the ground just ahead of them exploded with bullets hitting rock. They scrambled backward behind the cover of their original boulder.

"Well. That was fun," he panted.

H.O.T. Watch cut in, "Shooters moving fast in your direction."

Casey retorted, "Let me know when they reach the SUVs."

"Roger. SUVs in five…four…three…two…one…"

Boom.

Hake jumped, but was grinning before he landed back on the dirt. That was his girl. She'd managed to rig both vehicles to blow up without the terrorists spotting it. But then she yelled, "Run!" and he had no more time to think. He leaped up and took off running after her.

That fifty-foot open area took a dozen lifetimes to race across. With every step, the back of his neck braced for hot lead to rip through it. But then Casey took a running dive in front of him and he followed suit. He landed in a relatively soft patch of sand behind a low outcropping of sharp, volcanic rock.

Casey panted, "Catch your breath and then we'll start working our way up into the rocks. Maybe we'll get lucky and find a cave."

He nodded, too winded to speak.

Another voice intruded inside his head. The guy from H.O.T. Watch again. "We have movement in the south ridge opposite your position. Range three hundred yards. Eight hostiles moving on foot. Another dozen are circling wide to your left. Looks like they're planning to flank you and approach you from behind."

"Can we beat them over the ridge at our back?" Casey asked tersely.

"Negative."

"How much longer till that aerial drone gets here?" she demanded.

"Twelve minutes."

Hake frowned. It didn't take a military expert to know they were in trouble.

"Options?" Casey asked as she looked around, studying their position.

"Best bet is to hide," H.O.T. Watch replied.

Hake shook his head. "These are locals, if I had to bet. They'll know every nook and cranny of these mountains. It's likely the reason they chose this place for the handoff. We won't be able to hide from them."

Casey winced. "Unfortunately, Hake's right. How long until these guys are on top of us?"

The man replied, "Five to seven minutes at current speed. If you shoot at them, pin them down a little, you might stretch that to ten."

"Or they could just decide to run full-out at us and be here in three," she retorted.

She had a point. Hake looked around. They weren't in a good spot. Hostiles in front of them, a steep ridge about to be crawling with hostiles to their left and rear and only the gorge on their right. The gorge... "Casey, what if we go down instead of up?" he asked.

She frowned at him, then glanced at the gaping blackness on their right. "Go over the cliff? It's a thought. Let's have a look."

She took off crawling on her belly like an alligator, and

he imitated the movement. In about five seconds, his arms and back were protesting even though he was in pretty darned good shape. Meanwhile, Casey slithered along effortlessly in front of him. He caught up to her when she paused, her head jutting over the edge of a drop-off that made him light-headed to look at. The gorge yawned before him with nearly vertical walls. It might as well have been the Grand Canyon. No way could they climb down there.

"It's perfect," Casey announced.

He stared over at her. "Are you out of your mind? This is a sheer cliff. We'll kill ourselves if we try to climb it."

"That's why we're not climbing it. You'll jump."

"Are you mad?" he burst out.

She grinned. "Certifiably." As he stared in open disbelief, she added, "I've got a rappelling harness and cable. You'll put it on and go over the edge. I'll stay here and cover our position."

"I don't think so," he snapped. "You'll wear the harness and go over the edge, and I'll stay here to cover you."

"Hake, you're the civilian I'm here to protect. You're going down there. Besides, if I stay here, I can shoot at the bad guys until they take the truck and leave."

"I love you and take responsibility for you. I'll protect you."

She glared at him. "This isn't open to discussion."

"You're right," he replied grimly. "It's not."

Chapter 18

Casey stared at Hake in total exasperation. Did he have to go all macho and stubborn on her now? They didn't have time for this. She had to find a decent anchor point for her rappelling line, get him in the harness and make sure he knew how to use it. And she had about two minutes to make all of that happen.

"I'm not arguing with you about this—" she started.

He cut her off. "Good. Then don't. I'm done with you treating me like a helpless child you have to look after. I'm neither helpless nor a child. I knew what I was getting into when I came out here, and I was willing to do it to protect the people I love. And that includes you."

"I appreciate that, and I love you, too. But it doesn't change my mission parameters, which include protecting you."

The mission or her feelings for him—which was motivating her the most, she couldn't say. She supposed it didn't really matter. Either way, he was going over that cliff and she was staying behind.

"Listen to me, Casey. You've spent a good chunk of your adult life sacrificing your personal feelings for the job. And it's time to stop. You have a right to a life of your own. To happiness. Love. Quit being so damned noble and let me do this for you!"

"This is who I am," she ground out.

"And I love you for it. But part of loving someone is letting them love you back."

She stared at him, stunned. Was that her problem? She'd thought all along that she wasn't lovable. Not feminine enough or soft enough for any man. But was the problem really that she was incapable of letting anyone love her?

"Let me love you, Casey. I swear, it'll be worth the risk."

Risk. Now there was a word for it. Maybe she wasn't incapable of letting anyone love her. Maybe she was just afraid to. Terrified to the depths of her soul, in fact. Except this was Hake. He'd shown her over and over that he loved her and wanted to be with her, and she'd been too blinded by her own hang-ups to see it.

"What about you?" she challenged as she pulled her climbing gear out of her backpack and began untying it. "You're the one who keeps saying you don't do relationships. Why should I believe you?"

"People change. I've changed. Once I met you, I knew I'd be making the biggest mistake of my life if I let you get away from me. And I'm not a man who makes mistakes often."

"Why should I believe you?" Fear and denial swirled inside her, twisting around her heart like a pair of serpents.

"Because I love you. Because I want to spend the rest of my life with you. Because I'm asking you to marry me."

Marry him? Her entire being tumbled in confusion. He wanted to marry her? "But I'm a Hershey bar," she mumbled.

That damned voice from H.O.T. Watch intruded in her head again. "You're about to be a dead Hershey bar if you don't get moving."

He was right. She glared up at Hake. "We don't have time for this now. Put on this climbing harness." She shoved a jumble of webbing at him. "You step into these holes with your legs and buckle this part around your waist."

"I know how to use a climbing harness," he snapped. "And you're putting it on. You may ignore my marriage proposal, but you can't ignore the fact that I love you. I'd rather die than go on living without you." As she glared at him, he added implacably, "That's how I feel. Deal with it."

Damn him! Marriage and love and not living without her…it was heady stuff. Distracting stuff that would get them killed if she didn't get her mind back in the game and fast.

"How much do you weigh?" she asked abruptly.

"Two hundred pounds, give or take a couple. Why?"

"My cable's rated to two hundred fifty pounds. I weigh one-thirty. If I shed all my gear, we're eighty pounds over the max. That's about thirty percent. It might not work, but I'm willing to try us both riding down the cable."

He nodded briskly. "Done."

"You put on the harness. I'll ride on top of you," she ordered. "I'm lighter and have plenty of upper-body strength to hang on."

Thankfully, he grabbed the harness and yanked it over his feet.

"ETA on our hostiles?" she bit out.

H.O.T. Watch answered, "Three minutes. In about thirty seconds, the group at your twelve o'clock will come into the open. Suppression fire should be effective."

"Roger," she murmured. She pulled out her MP7 semi-automatic weapon and stretched out in a prone firing position. She began scanning the shadows before her.

"What can I do to help?" Hake asked quietly from beside her.

"You know how to shoot a weapon like this?" she asked.

"Yup. How about I provide cover fire while you tie off the rappelling cable."

"Perfect." She passed him the MP7. "Safety's off."

She inched backward, shocked to realize that she'd just entrusted him with a deadly weapon and her life and hadn't thought twice about it. He said he knew how to shoot and would cover her, and she believed him, no questions asked. Then why couldn't she believe him when he said he loved her and wanted to marry her?

She shoved the thought aside. They had to live through the next five minutes first, or the question would be moot. She looked around fast and spotted a solid-looking outcrop near the edge of the gorge. She made for it on her belly, catching a mouthful of dust and painful gravel down her shirt.

Bang! Hake had just shot behind her. Crud. The bad guys were almost here. As his pace of fire increased, she worked fast wedging crampons into crevices in the rocks and hammering them into place. She ran the end of the thin steel-and-titanium rappelling cable through all three tie-off points and secured it. If one crampon gave, the other two should hold. Assuming that any of this gear could take the extra thirty percent load they were about to put on it.

Bang! Bang, bang, bang. Hake was firing rapidly now, and H.O.T. Watch was calling out targets to him as fast as he could sight and fire at them.

"Hake!" she transmitted. "When I start firing, make your way over to me. Ready?"

"Yes," he grunted. "I'm almost out of ammo anyway."

"On my mark. Three...two...one...go!" she called as she started shooting her spare pistol at the moving shadows behind her. She ejected one clip and slammed in a second, resuming firing almost without pause. She had two more clips. Hake had to be at her side and ready to go by then, or they'd both die.

"Hurry," she gritted out as she continued firing grimly.

"Coming," he grunted, his voice strained with effort.

She slammed in her third clip. There seemed to be hostiles behind every rock out there, the muzzle flashes of their weapons pinpointing their positions. And then she caught a glimpse of something that made her blood run cold. More shadows swarming over the top of the ridge at her left.

Just a few more yards and Hake would reach her. She shoved in her last clip of ammo. But then she jumped as an explosion of noise erupted just in front of her. Hake was firing the MP7 one-handed as he crawled. It was actually damned hard to fire like that, but he sent a volley of lead up the slope, and the shadows momentarily stopped and ducked. She fired the last of her rounds over his back. Her pistol clicked. Empty.

"I'm out," he gasped.

She looked over her shoulder and swore. They still had a dozen feet of open space to cross prior to the cliff.

And then a new voice spoke in her head. "Need a little cover, Scorpion?"

Vanessa. And then her boss gave an order that warmed Casey all the way to her toes. "Fire at will, Medusas."

The night exploded into sound as a dozen high-powered weapons fired from across the gorge as expert markswomen unleashed hell's fury at the ridge behind her. "Time to go," she bit out.

She and Hake crawled low to the lip of the gorge. He lay down at the very edge of the cliff and she crawled on top of him, wrapping her arms tightly around his neck. Their gazes met in a moment of naked honesty that said it all. Fear, acceptance and, most of all, love passed between them in that instant.

The two of them had had a heck of a good run. If this was the end for both of them, there would be no regrets. Casey was stunned to see in his eyes the same gladness that he was here with her, like this. If he had to face death, he wanted to do it with her. Shockingly, she felt exactly the same way about him. And that was when she knew.

She truly loved him. This was the real deal.

He rolled to his side. Her legs came around his waist and she hung on to him for all she was worth.

"Don't you even think about letting go to sacrifice yourself for me," he muttered.

"Wouldn't dream of it."

His arms gripped her every bit as tightly as hers held him, and then they were falling, a sickening drop into space as the metal cable unwound from its holder with a metallic schwinging noise. They slammed into something hard, fetching up against the cliff face. She nearly lost her grip on Hake, but his arms tightened even more around her waist, crushing her against him.

They banged their way down the cliff face, tearing their clothes and getting scraped painfully. And then the cable tightened. The jerk of their fall breaking nearly dislodged her from Hake, despite both of them hanging on to each other with all their strength. Her legs came free, dangling in midair, and she scrabbled as her hands began to slip from around his neck, panicked. The abyss below beckoned.

"I've got you," he grunted, his arms tightening around her. She yanked her legs up and managed to get them wrapped around his waist once more. Thank God he was as big and strong as he was, or she'd have been a goner.

He leaned back in the harness, canting his body into a seated position within the webbing. She was able to rest much of her weight on his thighs as long as she maintained a good grip on him and kept her weight forward, close to his.

They spun in a slow circle, dangling under a small overhang.

"Seems like the cable's holding," he breathed.

"As long as the hostiles don't find our line and cut it, we might make it out of this," she breathed back.

Vanessa commented grimly, "Nobody's getting close to that line if I have anything to say about it. Report, Scorpion."

"So far so good," Casey replied.

The silence from above was nerve-wracking as she envisioned hostiles creeping toward the edge of the cliff to peer over. But then a faint sound reached her ears. Relief poured over her like a warm shower. That was the jet engine of an unmanned aerial vehicle. The drone was here.

"You are cleared to fire," the H.O.T. Watch controller announced after guiding the UAV to the far side of the ridge where the Medusas' weapons couldn't reach. A sound of automatic weapon fire erupted. *God bless the soldier on the other end of the drone's remote controller.* Shouts and the sounds of general chaos floated down into the gorge. Hake smiled at her, and she smiled back.

The drone made three passes overhead, and after the final one, another sound intruded upon the night. The engine of the truck Hake had brought to the meeting started up and the vehicle drove away. Silence fell once more.

"Did we make it?" Hake finally asked.

"We're not off this cable yet," she answered.

"Are we going to have to climb for it?" He looked doubtfully at the cliff behind them.

"We don't have the gear for a technical climb. A helicopter will have to come for us."

"How long is that going to take?" he asked.

She calculated the distance to the nearest U.S. Navy ship. "It could be an hour. Are you going to be okay for that long?"

"I'd hang here for a week if it meant you and me getting home alive," he declared.

She laid her head on his shoulder for a moment as the adrenaline of the immediate threat to their lives drained away, leaving her mostly tired and a lot scared. She knew the fear for what it was. Aftermath. Her mind was trained to hold off all emotions until the threat was over, and then, when the crisis was past, the feelings all came pouring in at once.

Except tonight, a host of other emotions came flooding in as well. Disbelief. Dismay. Joy. Exultation. Had Hake really proposed to her? Told her he'd rather die than live without her?

Caution—or maybe more of her same-old fear and unwillingness to let anyone get close to her—kicked in. Maybe that had just been Hake's adrenaline talking. He'd been facing death, and maybe he'd just blurted that stuff out by way of stress relief. She felt herself beginning to pull back emotionally. Dammit, she was going to lose him if she kept this up! She forcibly halted her retreat and asked in a small voice, "Did you mean what you said before?"

"About what?"

"About marrying me. And that stuff about preferring to die than go on without me?"

"Yes to both," he replied grimly. "For better or worse, that's how I feel."

"You're sure it wasn't just stress talking? I mean I'm fine if you just said all that to distract yourself from the fact that we were about to die."

"Casey, love?"

"What?"

"You think too much."

"I do not—"

He interrupted gently, "Yes, you do. Can't you just stop thinking for one minute and pay attention to how you feel?"

"Feelings are bad in my work."

"They happen to be an excellent thing in the rest of your life. Do you love me, Casey?"

"I…"

"Don't think about it. Just answer. Do you love me?" he challenged.

"Yes."

"Do you want to be with me?"

"Yes."

"Forever?"

"Yes."

"There, now. That wasn't so hard, was it?" he asked, laughing. "Someone will come get us off this rope and we'll go home, get married and live happily ever after."

"What?" she squawked. "I didn't say I'd marry you."

"Yes, you did. You said you love me and you want to be with me forever. What is marriage if it's not that?"

"But…you…me…*marriage?*" she squeaked.

"For a brave woman, you can sure be a giant chicken," he teased.

She stuck her tongue out at him. But he had a point. Love was a huge risk. It took courage. More than she had? And then she mentally snorted. She was a Medusa. Since when did a Medusa run from anything scary? Even if it was the prospect of handing her heart over into the keeping of a man? But not just any man. Hake. Did she trust him? Did she dare?

A faint thwocking noise became audible in the distance.

"I do believe our ride is here," Hake murmured.

More than a ride. The end of her mission. Return to her regularly scheduled life. She gazed at Hake, pained. He'd go back to his world of aggressive women and opulent excess, and she'd return to slogging around in jungles.

The thought left her completely, one-hundred-percent cold.

She jolted. Had he ruined her for ever being a Medusa again? A dark shape became visible, flying up down the gorge toward them.

If only she could have both—her military career and Hake. Then everything would be perfect. And that was when what he'd been trying to say to her all along hit her. She *could* have both. All she had to do was give herself permission.

The gunship made several passes out of sight, efficiently cleaning out the last resistance with its fifty-caliber machine gun. The helicopter came back one last time, easing into position overhead. She gripped Hake tightly as the rotor downwash did everything in its power to tear them apart. One last time, they clung to one another with all their strength.

A heavy hook swung tantalizingly beside them, and Hake reached out with one hand to snatch at it. It took him three hair-raising tries, but he finally grabbed it and hooked it onto his climbing harness. His arms went around her once more.

This was it. The end of the line. Literally and figuratively. Hake jolted beneath her and they began to rise.

"Fine!" she shouted. "I'll do it."

"Do what?" he shouted back.

"I'd rather jump off a cliff with you than lose you. How scary can marriage be after that?"

And that was how the two of them ended up tumbling onto the floor of the helicopter, tangled in one another's arms, kissing each other as if nothing else in the entire world existed but the two of them.

"I love you, Casey."

"And I love you, Hake."

"Are you ready for the adventure to begin?" he asked, grinning.

"I thought it just ended."

"Oh, no," he laughed. "We're just getting started."

* * * * *

*See below for a sneak peek from our classic
Harlequin® Romance® line.*

Introducing DADDY BY CHRISTMAS by Patricia Thayer.

MIA caught sight of Jarrett when he walked into the open
lobby. It was hard not to notice the man. In a charcoal
business suit with a crisp white shirt and striped tie covered
by a dark trench coat, he looked more Wall Street than
small-town Colorado.

Mia couldn't blame him for keeping his distance. He
was probably tired of taking care of her.

Besides, why would a man like Jarrett McKane be
interested in her? Why would he want to take on a woman
expecting a baby? Yet he'd done so many things for her.
He'd been there when she'd needed him most. How could
she not care about a man like that?

Heart pounding in her ears, she walked up behind him.
Jarrett turned to face her. "Did you get enough sleep last
night?"

"Yes, thanks to you," she said, wondering if he'd thought
about their kiss. Her gaze went to his mouth, then she
quickly glanced away. "And thank you for not bringing up
my meltdown."

Jarrett couldn't stop looking at Mia. Blue was definitely
her color, bringing out the richness of her eyes.

"What meltdown?" he said, trying hard to focus on what
she was saying. "You were just exhausted from lack of
sleep and worried about your baby."

He couldn't help remembering how, during the night,
he'd kept going in to watch her sleep. How strange was
that? "I hope you got enough rest."

She nodded. "Plenty. And you're a good neighbor for

coming to my rescue."

He tensed. Neighbor? *What neighbor kisses you like I did?* "That's me, just the full-service landlord," he said, trying to keep the sarcasm out of his voice. He started to leave, but she put her hand on his arm.

"Jarrett, what I meant was you went beyond helping me." Her eyes searched his face. "I've asked far too much of you."

"Did you hear me complain?"

She shook her head. "You should. I feel like I've taken advantage."

"Like I said, I haven't minded."

"And I'm grateful for everything…"

Grasping her hand on his arm, Jarrett leaned forward. The memory of last night's kiss had him aching for another. "I didn't do it for your gratitude, Mia."

Gorgeous tycoon Jarrett McKane has never believed in Christmas—but he can't help being drawn to soon-to-be-mom Mia Saunders! Christmases past were spent alone…and now Jarrett may just have a fairy-tale ending for all his Christmases future!

Available December 2010, only from Harlequin® Romance®.

HARLEQUIN®

A Romance

FOR EVERY MOOD™

Spotlight on
Classic

Quintessential, modern love stories
that are romance at its finest.

See the next page
to enjoy a sneak peek from
the Harlequin® Romance series.

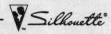

SPECIAL EDITION

USA TODAY BESTSELLING AUTHOR

MARIE FERRARELLA

BRINGS YOU ANOTHER
HEARTWARMING STORY FROM

When Lilli McCall disappeared on him
after he proposed, Kullen Manetti swore
never to fall in love again. Eight years later
Lilli is back in his life, threatening to break
down all the walls he's put up to
safeguard his heart.

UNWRAPPING
THE PLAYBOY

*Available December
wherever books are sold.*

REQUEST YOUR FREE BOOKS!

2 FREE NOVELS PLUS 2 FREE GIFTS!

Silhouette

ROMANTIC
SUSPENSE

Sparked by Danger, Fueled by Passion.

YES! Please send me 2 FREE Silhouette® Romantic Suspense novels and my 2 FREE gifts (gifts are worth about $10). After receiving them, if I don't wish to receive any more books, I can return the shipping statement marked "cancel." If I don't cancel, I will receive 4 brand-new novels every month and be billed just $4.24 per book in the U.S. or $4.99 per book in Canada. That's a saving of 15% off the cover price! It's quite a bargain! Shipping and handling is just 50¢ per book.* I understand that accepting the 2 free books and gifts places me under no obligation to buy anything. I can always return a shipment and cancel at any time. Even if I never buy another book from Silhouette, the two free books and gifts are mine to keep forever.

240/340 SDN E5Q4

Name _____ (PLEASE PRINT)

Address _____ Apt. #

City _____ State/Prov. _____ Zip/Postal Code

Signature (if under 18, a parent or guardian must sign)

Mail to the Silhouette Reader Service:

IN U.S.A.: P.O. Box 1867, Buffalo, NY 14240-1867
IN CANADA: P.O. Box 609, Fort Erie, Ontario L2A 5X3

Not valid for current subscribers to Silhouette Romantic Suspense books.

Want to try two free books from another line?
Call 1-800-873-8635 or visit www.morefreebooks.com.

* Terms and prices subject to change without notice. Prices do not include applicable taxes. N.Y. residents add applicable sales tax. Canadian residents will be charged applicable provincial taxes and GST. Offer not valid in Quebec. This offer is limited to one order per household. All orders subject to approval. Credit or debit balances in a customer's account(s) may be offset by any other outstanding balance owed by or to the customer. Please allow 4 to 6 weeks for delivery. Offer available while quantities last.

Your Privacy: Silhouette is committed to protecting your privacy. Our Privacy Policy is available online at www.eHarlequin.com or upon request from the Reader Service. From time to time we make our lists of customers available to reputable third parties who may have a product or service of interest to you. If you would prefer we not share your name and address, please check here. ☐

Help us get it right—We strive for accurate, respectful and relevant communications. To clarify or modify your communication preferences, visit us at www.ReaderService.com/consumerchoice.

SRS10R